Was the Funeral Fun?

A Novel

By

Anne Russ & Nancy Russ

This book is a work of fiction. Places, events, and situations in this story are purely fictional. Any resemblance to actual persons, living or dead, is coincidental.

ISBN: 1-4033-7201-2 (e-book)
ISBN: 1-4033-7202-0 (Paperback)
ISBN: 1-4033-8538-6 (Hardcover)

This book is printed on acid free paper.

1stBooks – rev. 10/23/02

Russwrites
3 Silver Maple Court
Little Rock, AR 72212

russwrite1@aol.com
russwrite2@aol.com

Dedication

This book is dedicated to
John Russ
Husband/Father of the authors
and a good story teller

And to the memory of
Katie Philley
Our mother/grandmother
Who is sharing her stories
With the Angels

"Was the funeral fun?"

He asks the same question about every funeral, and he always phrases the question just that way. He claims there is no appropriate way to inquire about a funeral, so it's easier just to be inappropriate.

He's right about that one. What are you supposed to say when, on your return from the funeral of a loved one, someone asks, "How was the funeral?"

Don't you just want to scream "It was really, really sad, you moron! Someone died. How do you think it was?"

Conversation between Lu Gibbs and her boyfriend.

CHAPTER 1

It was a slow day at the funeral home. In this line of work, we tend to look favorably upon down time. It may be the way I make a living, but I can't get too pumped up when the funeral business is "booming."

I had just about decided to take the afternoon off to enjoy a beautiful Arkansas fall day when Beulah Terwilleger and her husband, Ed, came in and announced that they were ready to pre-plan. They didn't have an appointment; but there was no other pressing business, so I ushered them into my office. It had just recently gotten cool enough to turn off the air conditioning and let the open window provide the cooling system. My office smelled fresh and clean—more like spring than fall.

Beulah's sister had recently passed away in Texas with no arrangements made, and her three children had quite a row about how the funeral should be handled.

"She's been gone for six months, and they're still not speaking to each other," Beulah said. "I would just die if that happened to my babies."

Beulah and Ed always remind me of the nursery rhyme:

> Jack Sprat could eat no fat
> His wife could eat no lean
> And so between them both, you see
> They licked the platter clean.

Her portly frame has a good 50 pounds on his; and when her jet-black, drugstore-dyed hair is at its peak, she stands at least five inches taller than he. Ed's a small, quiet guy. I imagine he still has hair, but I can't be sure since I never see him without a John Deere cap on his head. I assume he takes the cap off for church on Sunday; but since the Terwillegers are Baptists and I attend the Methodist church (when I can drag myself out of bed), I've never seen his pate *sans chapeau*. The Terwillegers really are a bit cartoonish looking. I had little doubt as to who would be deciding these arrangements.

1

Here at Gibbs Funeral home, when we pre-plan, we go the whole nine yards—casket, burial plot, type of flowers, music. My grandfather, Ernest Gibbs was actually one of the pioneers of the pre-plan concept back in the 30s, and he prides himself on leaving no stone unturned.

All the plans went smoothly until we got to the music part. You see, Beulah is our town singer. It's not an official title, but over the years people have been known to refer to her by that moniker. Beulah grew up in Chicago. She got "drafted" into a USO troupe during the Korean war right out of high school and had visions of a dazzling career in show biz. But she met Ed on one of her tours, and after the war she married him and they came back to Hilltop. Ed inherited his father's farm equipment and repair business and did well even after farmers started going bust. No matter how poor a farmer is he's got to have equipment that runs.

Anyway, Beulah's visions of fame and fortune got a little fuzzy after five kids, and she became quite content with being Hilltop's premier song stylist. Though her voice is not quite what it used to be, she still belts out a rendition of *Because* at most of the weddings in town and provides her version of *Abide With Me* or *Amazing Grace* at all the town funerals. For those who want something a little more highbrow, she can sing *The Lord's Prayer*—it fits either occasion. Basically, it's not considered a ceremony in Hilltop unless Beulah sings.

So you can see the problem we were up against. Who would sing at Beulah's funeral? Ed's too. Beulah claimed she would be far too grief stricken to squeak out even one little note if Ed were to beat her to the Pearly Gates. (I could almost hear Ed lift up a silent prayer at that statement). Now, of course, Beulah is not the only person in Hilltop who can carry a tune. There's little Mary Margaret at the high school. She has a beautiful voice and stars in all the community theater productions. Beulah nixed Mary Margaret for her funeral because Mary Margaret is Catholic, and Beulah was afraid she might sing *Ave Maria*.

"Over my dead body," Beulah said, without a trace of irony in her voice.

Bob Franken, the music director at the Episcopal Church has a beautiful voice, but his taste in music is different from Beulah's (probably from most of our clients'). I can't imagine him singing "Beyond the Sunset," which is a favorite funeral solo here.

Finally Ed, who had remained silent for the last half-hour spoke up. "Why don't we make a recording of you singing, Muffin? Then you can sing at both funerals."

The look on Beulah's face was that of a person who has just realized she can have her cake and eat it too.

"That's a wonderful idea, Ed," she cried. "I'll just borrow Amelia's karaoke machine and make a tape! That way I don't have to settle for a second-rate singer at my funeral. You either, Ed."

Ed looked relieved. Whether it was because he felt assured Beulah's voice would be heard at his funeral or because our meeting could now conclude I'll never know. I was just happy to have solved yet another potential "funeral obstacle" for the folks seated in front of me. I'm starting to get pretty good at this.

Grandpa has run Gibbs Funeral Home in Hilltop, Arkansas for 70 years. No, that's not a typo. He's 92 years old and still comes to work every day. The only time he ever even missed a funeral was back in the summer of '90 when we were having that awful heat wave. That was the summer the Humane Society got all up in arms because the favorite activity for boys between the ages of five and 14 was to dig for earthworms and then set them out on the pavement to watch them fry. Anyway, right in the middle of one of the worst of the worm-frying days, Grandpa had a graveside service to preside over. Doc Green told him if he went out in the 100-plus temperature, the next funeral he attended would be his own.

Since I came to work for Grandpa, people in Hilltop have had to adjust to the idea of a "girl" funeral director. Actually, folks here still call us "undertakers." It's probably the most descriptive term for what we actually do, but I must say I prefer the more modern, politically correct, title of funeral director.

Not that I'm anything like what people see as a "typical" funeral director. Besides being female, I'm a little more than a year away from turning 30, and I carry a long mane of flaming red hair with me everywhere I go—somber looking, I'm not.

I was born here, but I left Hilltop after high school to go to college. I decided I hadn't learned enough in four years (actually I couldn't find a job), so I went on to get my master's in social work.

3

Armed with impressive credentials, I headed to the big city of St. Louis to seek fame and fortune as a counselor for disadvantaged and disturbed youth. These kids had seen and done enough to last ten lifetimes. I lasted two-and-a-half years, which is a year longer than the average program employee in that job.

When I'd had my fill of the big city and the daunting problems of today's urban youth, I decided to come home and go into the family business. I couldn't have given Grandpa a better present.

Dad and his brother Billy never were much interested in the dead. Actually, Dad hasn't been interested in much of anything since Mom ran off with the music minister from Calvary Baptist Church when I was eight years old. Dad went into a funk, and I went into the refrigerator. Neither of us has ever really come out of our refuges. Dad holes up at the local Mercantile Bank doling out loans to the few people who come in requesting them; and when he's not in his cell, you can find him digging in his gardens around the house. At 5'8, I am a zaftig size 16 and am coming to terms with the fact that I will never be a supermodel.

I have to thank Rosie for the fact that I'm finally OK with my less-than-svelte figure—Rosie O'Donnel, the comedienne turned talk show host. I feel like we're kindred spirits. Her mom died when Rosie was about 10, and she says she turned to food for comfort. I know that her mom died and my mom left, but gone is gone—doesn't much matter to an eight-year-old.

A lot of folks have the misconception that people who are involved in the funeral business are fascinated by the dead. That's simply not true. Most of us are much more concerned with the living. That's who we're here for. People come to us at the lowest point of their lives. They've lost a loved one. You'd think that here in the buckle of the Bible belt death wouldn't be so hard on the ones left behind. I mean, if we all truly believe what we claim about Jesus being the Resurrection and the Life, then we should rejoice that our loved ones have moved from this world full of heavy burdens to a new one filled with peace and light. I don't care what some preachers say, it just doesn't work that way. No matter how wonderful a place we believe our loved ones are in now, they're not here with us anymore—and that hurts.

I don't actually do anything to the bodies. My cousin Mo handles that. A few years back, he went over to the community college at Haven to get his mortician's license. Mo was born Maurice, thanks to my Aunt Letitia. Letitia is the daughter of a wealthy rice farmer. She has a degree in French from William Woods, an all-girls college in Missouri. After college, she came back to Hilltop and set her cap for my Uncle Billy. She named her children Maurice and Francois. Maurice has settled down in the family business, and Francois makes a very good living as a designer of high-end bathrooms in the Dallas/Ft. Worth area. Francois doesn't come home often because the love of his life—Tim—is not welcome in Aunt Lettie's house.

Funerals are a very touchy subject, and pre-planning is even touchier. People don't like to think about their own mortality, much less talk about it. Making all the arrangements ahead of time is actually a very selfless act. It gives the people left behind a little less to worry about while they are dealing with their grief.

One of my first funeral pre-planning cases was Mrs. Michael McCafferty (Mary Mac to her friends). She wasn't really thrilled with having to deal with me. She thought anyone involved in planning a funeral ought to be "old enough to die themselves." I assured her that any of us could die at any time. (I think I made a crack about life being a terminal illness, but it didn't help the situation. Death jokes don't play well in a funeral home.) Like most of our funerals, Mrs. McCafferty's service would be held at the church of her choice. For Mary Mac, this was the First Methodist Church on Main Street where she has taught Sunday School for so many years everyone has lost count.

She wanted an open casket, unless her demise was brought on by a disfiguring accident. We keep a hair and make-up stylist under contract (Emily down at the Beauty Box), but Mary Mac made plans to have her stylist from Plainview come over to do her hair.

"Nobody but Joel knows how to do it."

Mary Mac is from the old school. She gets her hair shampooed, rolled and set every week and doesn't touch it until her next standing appointment. I figured as long as her passing didn't involve a tumble down the stairs or some sort of boating accident, her hair would pretty much remain intact; but I didn't bring that up.

My grandfather taught me that we must do our best to honor a funeral request no matter how bizarre it is.

"Death is a sacred and a scary thing," he says. "By assuring people that their wishes will be carried out after their death, we give them a little extra peace in life."

Today, I hoped that the Terwillegers were leaving our office with a little extra sense of peace—especially Ed.

CHAPTER 2

I was escorting the Terwillegers to the door when the phone rang. Mo answered but promptly handed the phone over to me.

"Lu, it's Molly. I think Dad's dead," she said in a very calm voice. Then she began sobbing hysterically over the phone.

Molly Morehouse is a school teacher over at the high school. Just about the time she and Frank got their two kids off to college, her mother died; and she felt her father shouldn't live alone. When Mr. Kirby arrived five years ago, he was in good health and good spirits. He and several other men played dominoes in front of the town hall when the weather was seasonable. He was a charmer, and that made him a much-sought-after companion by the many widows in our community. Someone had him over for a meal every Friday and Saturday night and Sunday after church. He was quite the man-about-town. About six months ago, he had a light stroke. It didn't leave him paralyzed but seemed to zap him of his vim and vigor.

"Molly, have you called Doc Green?" I asked in my best calm, it-will-be-all right-voice.

"No," she said, gulping back sobs. "I didn't know what to do. When I went in this morning to wake him for breakfast, he wasn't breathing and there was no pulse."

She was beginning to hyperventilate now.

"Molly, I'll call Doc Green, and we'll both be over there as soon as possible. Just try to sit tight until then. Is Frank there with you?" I asked.

"No, he's already gone to work."

"Get a paper bag and breathe into it until you calm down. Then call Frank and have him come home," I told her. "Mo and I will be right there."

I hung up, praying she wouldn't pass out before we got there, and went to find Mo.

Mo is the most elegant big man I've ever seen. At 6'4" and 210 pounds, he should be a hulking figure; but he's really rather graceful. His movements are all very fluid, and even his sandy brown hair just sort of falls in waves around his face. He's the kind of person who always looks neat, even in jeans and a T-shirt. He has always been a person—even when he was a child. He's about four years younger than I but he has always seemed so—I don't know—wise, I guess. Like when we were kids and the church took us all to the local nursing home to sing at Christmas time. Lord have mercy, were we awful! Anyway, the rest of us were a little afraid of all the frail, old people in this building that smelled funny. But Mo walked right up to every one of them—even the ones who were disoriented or disfigured—and gave out great big hugs.

In spite of the fact that he was a big hugger as a child, Mo is actually very shy. When we get a call to pick up a body, he rarely says a word. He just stays in the background with his hands clasped in front of him. What he lacks in ability to make small talk with the living, he makes up for by his treatment of those who have ceased to live. Mo takes great pride in his work. He and Emily Peartree pore over pictures of the deceased. And since they know most of the folks who come through our doors, they spend at least an hour talking about the deceased—how much he liked to golf, or the great pride she took in her award-winning cherry pie recipe. They do everything they can to make sure the dead look the way they did in life.

In contrast to Mo, Emily is our funeral home firecracker. I love having her around. She is a tiny little freckle-faced girl with tons of energy and impeccably groomed fingernails. Even when she's standing still, you get the feeling she's in motion. I think it's her curly brown hair that just sort of bobs around her face when she talks (which is almost constantly). I guess that's why she and Mo work together so well—she talks; he listens.

Most folks around here don't even know how good Mo is. They think the dead are supposed to look the same way they always did—only sleeping. But those who have traveled out of town for open-casket services or viewings are always astonished at how unnatural the dearly departed actually look without my cousin's help.

"He just looked, well, he just looked so dead!" Myrtle Talbot told me when she and her husband returned from his father's funeral in another state. "And he was such a lively man."

Mo simply remembers that everyone who ends up on his table is loved and will be missed by someone. He wants that someone to be able to remember his or her loved one the way he or she was and not disguised by cheap pancake makeup and too much hairspray. If you don't find Mo's devotion to his work a tad creepy, it's really quite sweet.

Mo followed my little Honda in the hearse to the Morehouse home. We went in without knocking and found Molly in the kitchen. A bottle of Old Crow and a half-empty tumbler on the counter caught my attention. I've never seen Molly drink anything stronger than a glass of champagne at a wedding—and even that made her a little giddy. She is normally the picture of poise and perfection. She wears her chestnut brown hair in a page boy flip that looks exactly like it did in her senior yearbook picture. I've never once seen her in public without earrings and fresh lipstick. Today, all bets were off. Her hair was a mess; her eyes were puffy from crying; and her face (including her lips) were ghostly pale.

"Molly, where did you get this?" I asked, alluding to the Old Crow bottle.

She blubbered, "I bought it about three years ago for this marvelous pork loin recipe I heard on Martha Stewart. You remember I served it at that engagement dinner party for Sherry and that boy she married from somewhere up north. It was to die for. I don't know why I never made it again. Do you think it's still good?" she asked as she finished up the glass and proceeded to pour another.

Just then Frank walked in the door.

"Molly! What's happened? Are you alright?"

Apparently, Frank had merely received a page at work that instructed him to come home right away. He arrived to find a hearse in the driveway and his wife in the kitchen throwing back cheap liquor like it was lemonade.

"Dad's dead!" Molly cried and threw her arms around her husband's neck.

That outburst brought me back to reality. I had become so discombobulated at finding Molly in such a state that I forgot we were not here for a social call. Mo, of course, had been standing quietly in a corner with his hands folded waiting for the hysteria to subside. Leaving Frank and Molly in the kitchen, we went in search of Mr. Kirby. We found him in his bedroom, lying peacefully. Mo confirmed that he had indeed expired, but we weren't going to move anything until Doc Green arrived to sign the death certificate.

I reflected on how fortunate Mr. Kirby was. With all our glorious medical technology, hardly anyone dies at home anymore. Unfortunately, most of us will spend our last hours, or days, in a hospital or nursing home bed, often hooked up to some hideous machinery. To say goodnight to loved ones and then "go gently into that good night" is really the best any of us can hope for.

My ruminations on life and death were interrupted by the arrival of Doc Green. The good doctor agreed with Mo that Mr. Kirby had breathed his last. Molly came in to say a final goodbye, and Doc Green helped Mo cover the body and put him on the gurney. Doc Green followed Mo back to the funeral home, and I stayed behind to talk with Molly and Frank.

A funeral director has many roles. Because most of our "customers" are also friends, my grandfather and I often go beyond the call of duty. While Frank was brewing some coffee in an attempt to sober Molly up, I got on the phone and called their minister and the chairwoman of the ladies auxiliary at their church. (You wouldn't believe the numbers a small-town funeral director keeps in her trusty Filofax).

The last call was possibly the most important. The Ladies Auxiliary will mobilize. When someone in their congregation is touched by any sort of tragedy, the members are on the case. Prayers are said, arrangements made, and of course, food is brought.

When someone dies, people need to do something for the ones left behind. The truth is, there's not a whole lot you can do; but nobody likes to feel helpless. In the South, we have an answer to that problem—food.

I guarantee that by tomorrow morning the Morehouse kitchen will be filled to the brim with everything anyone could possibly want to eat. I can even predict what there will be to choose from.

> *Homemade Bread—always a crowd pleaser. It shows you took the time to make something especially for them (breadmaker bread is acceptable, but from scratch is preferred).*
>
> *Cobbler—with so many varieties, chances are no one else will bring exactly the same kind. Cobbler can*

also be heated and reheated, or eaten cold, depending on one's mood.

Finger Sandwiches—part of the reason for bringing food is to feed the many visitors who will come in to offer condolences. Finger sandwiches offer something for everyone, and they make little mess.

Meat and Cheese trays—while these lack that personal touch, they are one of the first items to be consumed. Variety and low-mess factor make deli trays a funeral favorite.

Casseroles—probably the number one funeral food here in Hilltop. The variations on a theme that can be created with a chunk of Velveeta and a box of Ritz Crackers are positively endless. Currently, Mattie Bennet's broccoli, rice and cheese casserole is considered the best recipe in town, so it'll be the first to go. Beulah Terwilleger also makes a tasty version with ham and green peas, and I know for a fact she resents that Mattie's always gets eaten first.

Bucket of Chicken—sounds a little impersonal, but if there are likely to be little ones around, fried chicken is just the thing. Just be sure to bring plenty of napkins. You don't want greasy handprints on the furniture and drapes.

There's nearly always more food than everybody can eat, but it can be frozen for consumption at a later date. In addition to food, friends bring big supplies of paper products. Most southerners know that certain occasions just call for the convenience of disposable dishes.

Confident that everyone had been called, and that Frank wasn't going to allow Molly to polish off the bottle of whiskey, I was headed out the door when Brother Toomey drove up. Thad Toomey is the only minister in town who wears a Cardinals baseball jacket more often than he wears a tie. He's not quite 30; and he and his wife, Tori, have twin boys.

The Morehouses belong to the "liberal" Baptist Church in town where Thad occupies the pulpit. When I was a little girl, Calvary was the only Baptist Church in town, but years ago there was a big split.

At the time, the big issue seemed to be whether women should be allowed to wear pants to church. It was the late 70s, and the women's movement was just hitting Hilltop. The controversy was really between those people who took the Bible literally and those that didn't, but all the actual arguments were over women and pants. (Looking back, I think all the hoopla was a diversionary tactic to make folks forget that the music minister they loved and trusted had run off with another man's wife, *aka*, my mom) Nevertheless, the church split. Members of the contingent who objected to "women in pants" formed a separate church. For the longest time Calvary Baptist was referred to as The Baptist Church and the new church (Second Baptist) was simply called The Other One.

I could tell Thad was psyching himself up to go inside. Even though he is a minister, death is not Brother Toomey's strong suit. Actually, it's not death he has a problem with—it's the people left behind that make him uncomfortable. We've talked about it several times since he moved to Hilltop. Thad is one of those people who was truly called to the ministry. He's a fabulous preacher. He has the energy to keep up with the young people in his congregation and the patience and kindness to minister to his elderly parishioners as well. I know of at least three couples who give him credit for saving their marriages. However, he is not gifted when it comes to dealing with grief. Oh, he'll say the right things and offer comfort to Molly and Frank. But I know that when he leaves he's likely to go to bed with a migraine.

"I'll be in the office later this afternoon if you want to come by and talk," I told him.

He smiled and took a deep cleansing breath as he walked up the drive toward the house.

CHAPTER 3

Since I was out and about, I decided to go over and check on my investments with Uncle Billy. I'm not a big-time wheeler-dealer, but I do keep a pretty hefty IRA portfolio, and I dabble in a few stocks. While I have gone into the family business, I don't want to follow in my grandfather's footsteps and still be working when I'm 90. I don't want death to be my life.

Billy apparently has a gift for investing. He didn't even finish college. He just read some books and took a series of tests that certified him as a financial planner. Since he's made a lot of money, people trust him to manage their money.

Of course, my uncle didn't exactly start out with peanuts. Billy was home from college one summer and working for Sam's Construction Company. A forklift backed right over him while he was eating his sack lunch and broke both legs in several places. Turns out the forklift operator, who happened to be Sam's son-in-law, had been drinking on the job. Even before suing became a national pastime, Billy got himself a big city lawyer and a bundle of money. Three operations and two years of physical therapy later, Billy was able to walk as well as anyone—though his legs still ache something fierce when the weather gets damp. I've often wondered if he feels the trade-off was worth it.

About the time of Billy's $4.2 million windfall was when Letitia Wentworth started sniffing around him. Granted, this is the way Grandpa tells the story, and he never much cared for Letitia and her French. But according to him, when the first settlement check arrived, Letitia set her cap for my Uncle Billy quicker than you can say "punitive damages."

I can't say that I blame her. It was 1965, and the woman was living in Small Town, USA armed only with a degree in French and her good looks. A lot of people in town think Letitia is shallow and selfish. It's not that at all. Actually, she's very intelligent and feels things very deeply. She can be quite charitable. At funerals, most families are besieged with flowers for the deceased. We give them the option of leaving them at the grave site or donating them to shut-ins or people at the Shady Pines Rest Home. Letitia coordinates the flower runs. She either delivers them herself or makes sure someone from the Ladies Auxiliary does. She's always doing things for other people. When her boys were small, she never missed a Little League game or a band concert. No, Aunt Letty is not shallow—pretentious maybe. She's really a good person—she just thinks she's better than everyone else.

Aunt Letty is particularly nice to me on account of a tidbit of information I stumbled on a few years back. It's the kind of thing that I don't give a fig about, but Letty would be devastated if my currently private knowledge ever came to be made public.

Aunt Letty was actually in the office when I stopped by.

"Oh, hey, Lu. *Comment t'appelle-tu?* Did you need to see Billy? He's got a meeting in Mercer today with some new clients. Seems like someone over there has had a big settlement in an injury suit, and the family wants Billy to handle all their newfound wealth. *Quel suprise!* I'm just here answering the phones. Can I help you with something?"

All of this was said in one complete breath.

"No thanks, Aunt Letty. (Like most southerners, I still refer to relatives by the titles I used as a child even though we are all adults now.) "I just wanted to find out how some of my investments are doing. I'll catch him later."

"You and your daddy are still coming over for Sunday dinner after church?" she asked. "I'm making *le coq au vin* and chocolate mousse."

Regardless of what my Grandpa feels about Letitia and her French, the woman's cooking would rival any five-star restaurant in Paris. I can endure conversations peppered with foreign expressions as long as I keep getting invited to dinner.

"We'll be there," I said firmly and walked out the door before Letitia could let loose with an *au revoir.*

CHAPTER 4

The next day was a busy one. I spent the morning making arrangements for Molly's father, and Wendell Waltham's visitation was in the afternoon. Grandpa and Mo were going to get everything set up, but I felt like I should be there to offer condolences to the family. I wasn't even quite sure how Wendell had died. He was only about 65 and seemed pretty healthy to me. You never can tell—you learn that pretty quickly in the funeral home business.

The visitation room is to the right as you walk in the door. It's not huge, but it is outfitted with three couches and several armchairs so the family can be as comfortable as possible. It is decorated in rich greens and maroons. The lighting is soft—almost pink in hue. We pipe in some very soft music—not Muzak!—so soft that it's almost undetectable, like white noise. Every thing about the visitation room is designed to help people feel at ease. So often at a funeral, mourners come, sign a guest book, sit through the service and leave without ever speaking to the family. Visitation time means face to face contact. I've met only a handful of people in my life who always know the right thing to say in that situation. Everyone else has to wing it. And I've seen a couple crash and burn.

The worst exchange I've witnessed in the visitation room was right after I started work for Grandpa. One of the smaller churches had this new, young minister straight out of Bible College. He looked about twelve, was self-described as "on fire for the Lord," and had never set foot in a funeral home. The deceased was a middle-aged father of three who had died suddenly of a massive heart attack. Brother whoever-he-was took the widow by the hand and said, "As wonderful and as joyful a place as we know heaven is, aren't we all just better off dead?"

Nobody was shocked when the church called a new minister within the month.

When I arrived back at work, Miss Mattie was the first person I saw. In addition to her role as crowd-pleasing casserole chef, Mattie Bennet is part of what I call the go-and-sit crew from the Waltham family's church. Every church has a similar crew. They are generally comprised of retired people (mainly women) who sit at the funeral

15

home during the visitation period. They hold the hands of the grieving and offer up little nuggets of wisdom and comfort.

"I guess it was just his time."

"She led such a good life."

"God has called him home."

"Doesn't she look good in that dress?"

"The flowers are all so nice—and not a cheap one in the bunch."

"He was so full of life."

"She's in a better place."

And my favorite: "God needed him in Heaven."

In addition to being the ring leader of the go-and-sit crew from the Second Baptist Church, Miss Mattie is also the biggest gossip in town. She's lived 82 years in this town, and she knows everything about everyone and never forgets a thing. Fortunately, she is a good person, and she's not malicious. She just likes to share what she knows. She cornered me the minute I walked in the door.

"Such a terrible thing about Wendell, isn't it?" said Miss Mattie who, even with her snow-white beehive hair-do only comes up to my chin. "The drinking finally did him in."

The look on my face must have given me away. First of all, it's an unwritten rule not to speak ill of the dead, especially at the wake (very tacky). And second, I had no idea what she was talking about.

"Oh, you didn't know," Miss Mattie went on. "Yes, Wendell's been drinking ever since his family lost their money back in the early eighties. I've heard he had bottles hidden all over that falling-down house of his."

I had forgotten about that—the money, I mean. The Waltham's used to own the local grocery and hardware store. When I was in junior high, Hilltop got a Wal-Mart with a hardware section and a Kroger with a deli counter and bakery; and the Waltham's store eventually closed from the competition. People here like to be loyal to local businesses, but when you can cut your family grocery bill in half, devotion to protecting the small-town economy goes out the window.

"You know he never did get over his wife leaving him after the store shut down," Miss Mattie continued. "You remember Gertie, don't you? Pretty little thing, even if she did wear her make-up too heavy and her skirts too short, bless her heart."

(In the South a woman can get away with saying most anything about anyone as long as she follows it up with "Bless her heart." It kind of softens the blow and implies that you're not trying to be cruel, you're simply stating the plain, pitiful truth.)

"As soon as Wendell filed for bankruptcy, Gertie high-tailed it out of town with that surgeon from over at Jonesboro. Praise the Lord Wendell's parents weren't alive to see that. His mother was one of my dearest friends. Sweet woman. Made an absolutely divine casserole with tomato and eggplant. Anyway, he—the surgeon—had been coming to our hospital once a week to do routine surgeries. You know—tonsils, appendix and that kind of thing. They've quit doing that now. You have to get all invasive procedures done somewhere else these days. Anyway, I've heard that's when Wendell really dove into the bottle. Apparently vodka was his poison. You can't smell that on people, you know."

As my brain was processing this vast amount of unsolicited information, visitors began to come in. From time to time, Miss Mattie would interrupt her narrative long enough to say "Hello, how are you, dear?" or "I haven't seen you in ages, we'll have to catch up" to people coming in the door, but never long enough for me to make a graceful exit.

"I'm not surprised you didn't know," Mattie continued. "Most people didn't. Wendell knew how to keep a secret. Do you remember his second wife? Married a girl half his age. When she left, the story Wendell put out was that she was going back east to go to graduate school. What he didn't tell was that he was footing the entire Ivy League bill with what little money he had left in return for her silence. He couldn't have folks around here knowing that the real reason the child left was because one night in a drunken rage he dislocated her shoulder, knocked out a tooth and banged her head against the wall hard enough to give her a mild concussion."

I must have looked completely dumbfounded. I don't know what shocked me more—that mild-mannered Wendie was a closet alcoholic with a violent streak or that Miss Mattie knew all of this and was telling it to me not 10 feet from the poor man's body!

"I know it's a shock," said Miss Mattie, patting my hand. The hand pat is Miss Mattie's standard gesture of comfort. All the go-and-sit crew members have their own. Amelia Richardson puts one arm

17

around your shoulder. Beulah Terwilleger clasps your hand between both of hers and lets out a huge sigh. Vernon Dudley (one of the few male crew members) pats people on the back, continuously, like someone burping a baby. And our retired librarian Addy McGuire gives a full-out hug (don't let her diminutive size and soft voice fool you, she's been known to crack a rib or two).

I was all set to hear more about Wendell Waltham's not-so-secret life, when Miss Mattie dropped my hand and made a bee-line to a very attractive middle-aged woman. The woman looked like a model in a black dress that was so simple and elegant I knew it must have cost a fortune. That dress didn't come from Hilltop. The room was tiny, but she looked a little lost, like she wasn't quite sure what was happening here.

I heard Miss Mattie say "Glenda, it's been too long. And to think it took this to bring you back home."

Glenda. Glenda. Glenda. Aha! Glenda was Wendell's only sister, and I suppose his only living blood relative. I'd never met Glenda, but I had heard the stories. What was it she had done? Where had she been all these years? Then it hit me. She was the one who ran away with the circus! No, really. She did.

This all happened before I was born, but I remember people comparing my mother to Glenda when she took off.

"At least Glenda didn't leave a husband and child behind!"

I'm not quite up to par with Miss Mattie, but I do enjoy a good story. If I remember correctly, Glenda's high school sweetheart went off to Vietnam, and like so many others, didn't make it home. Glenda went completely catatonic when she heard the news. She literally didn't utter a sound for more than six months.

When Wendell heard the circus was coming to town, he thought the big top and the bright lights were the perfect antidote for what was ailing his little sister. Boy, was it ever! Somehow, Glenda managed to slip off from her older brother and make her way back to the dressing area. She ended up in the dressing room of Vladimir, World Famous Contortionist. The next time Wendell saw her she was in center ring with Vladimir—showing off talents that had apparently been hidden all her life. Good thing, too. Now stories do tend to become more extravagant each time they're told, but from what I've heard, some of the things Glenda and Vladimir did with their bodies in that ring could get you arrested in most states—at least the southern ones. The whole incident was fodder for a slew of off-color contortionist jokes that still make the rounds about town today.

When the circus left town, so did Glenda. She ran away with Vladimir and to my knowledge hasn't been seen in town until today. I haven't thought about the "Glenda" stories in ages. When I was a little girl, I thought it all sounded very romantic. She was sort of my hero—and here she was in the flesh.

Normally, I frown on eavesdropping, but I really should mingle with the other mourners. If I happened to get close enough to Glenda and Miss Mattie to overhear their conversation, then so be it.

"I can't believe you recognized me," Glenda said in a soft voice that hadn't lost its Southern drawl. "It's been nearly 30 years."

"Nonsense!" said Miss Mattie. "I would have known you anywhere. Is Yakov with you?"

Glenda looked puzzled, and then laughed.

"You mean Vladimir," she said. "No, after about three years he picked up a new partner in Tallahassee. She was double jointed. There was no way I could compete with that."

"Well what have you been up to all that time?" Miss Mattie countered.

"Oh, this and that," Glenda answered, sounding deliberately vague. "It was so nice of you to come. Wendie would have been so pleased with the turnout. If you'll excuse me, I must say hello to a few other people."

Clearly disgruntled, Miss Mattie went in search of others who might be able to shed a little more light on the life and times of Ms. Glenda Waltham—or whatever her name is now.

After making the rounds myself, I decided to go home and get a good night's sleep. We would have Wendell's funeral and burial tomorrow morning, and after that I had a lunch date scheduled with my one and only.

Anne Russ and Nancy Russ

CHAPTER 5

James Patrick Whirley, Jr. (Jim Pat to his friends) and I went to school together all our lives. He was a class ahead of me. Jim Pat was one of those nice guys who just kind of blended in. He made decent grades, played second string on the basketball team and was the preferred lawn mower of the greater Hilltop area. He was friends with everyone and never got into much trouble. Just a regular guy. When I got back into town and walked into Whirley's Family Pharmacy, you could have knocked me over with a feather. There, behind the counter, was Jim Pat—only better. I still can't put my finger on what has changed since high school. He doesn't look that different. Maybe his chest is a little broader. Or maybe his face is slightly more chiseled. His hair is definitely shorter. Whatever has happened, it works for me. As Rosie would say, he's a real cutie patootie.

Jim Pat runs the family pharmacy. He followed in the footsteps of his mother, not his father. Nancy Whirley was one of the first female pharmacists in the state. Originally a Whitney, Nancy comes from old money. Some folks say their family can trace its roots back to cotton gin king, Eli Whitney, but I don't know that it's ever been documented. Nancy's brother, Whit (yes, Whit Whitney), runs the bank the family started over 75 years ago.

Nancy snared James Patrick Whirley, Sr. while she was in college. I say "snared" because Mrs. Whirley is a very determined woman. I don't know of anything she's ever wanted that she didn't get. I just imagine that once she decided James Whirley was going to be hers, he didn't have much to say about the matter. I would also wager that if asked, Mr. Whirley would swear that he pursued her.

Regardless of who wooed whom, Nancy Whitney Whirley brought her husband back to her hometown. She opened the pharmacy, and he got a job as a social science teacher and coach at the local school. He started out coaching junior high volleyball and high school track. I remember him as an average history teacher, but his volleyball and track teams were winners. He started basketball and volleyball teams for the girls and even had girls running track. Coach Whirley is now the athletic director and head football coach at the high school, and practically every kid in school is involved in some kind of athletics. Who says there is no such thing as a career track in a small town?

Having a family business to inherit is not the only reason Jim Pat went into pharmacy. He had an older sister named Caroline. She was beautiful, was at the head of her class, and held the state tennis doubles title for two years running. She was also anorexic. When Jim Pat was 10 years old, she died. Caroline was seventeen.

I worked with some anorexics during my internship as a social worker. I was fascinated with what caused this disease—probably because I couldn't *not* eat if my life depended on it. As I learned more about why girls voluntarily starve themselves, I thought a lot about Caroline and why she did it. Maybe she felt she couldn't measure up to her trail-blazing, entrepreneurial mom. Maybe nobody ever told her how pretty and smart and talented she was. Maybe they did, and for some reason, she couldn't believe them.

Caroline's funeral was the first one I ever attended. At first it was rather pleasant. The sanctuary was filled with flowers. Bertha, of course, sang. It was a Catholic funeral, and I was fascinated with the robed priest who sprinkled incense and chanted over the casket. The priest and some of Caroline's friends stood and told wonderful stories about her. But then the pallbearers picked up the casket and started down the aisle with Jim Pat and his family following behind. That's when it hit me—Caroline wasn't coming back. This was it. A panic went through my body that I had never experienced before and have yet to experience again. The only person I'd ever lost was my mom, and one year after her departure I still clung to the hope that she would be back. I knew Caroline wouldn't.

I stayed off-balance the rest of the day. I remember the whole day very clearly, but like you remember a dream, not like you remember something you actually lived. This may sound corny, but I didn't feel all right until the sun came up the next morning. I sat on my bed and watched the sun rise outside my window. In my mind, what had happened the day before was the worst thing that could ever happen in life. Yet the world had somehow survived it, and I was still in the world. I don't know if my young mind processed it quite that way. All I know is, when I watched that sun come up, I felt like everything was going to be okay.

Jim Pat was okay, too. But Caroline's death changed his world forever. Not only did he lose his sister, but his parents blamed each other (and themselves) for what had happened. Good Catholics that they are, the Whirleys will never divorce; but I wouldn't say they have much of a marriage either.

Jim Pat got a degree in nutrition with a minor in psych before he went to pharmacy school. He goes into the classrooms of the junior high and high school to teach the kids (especially the girls) about good nutrition and feeling good about their bodies. Having a good-looking guy stand up and say that Kate Moss look-a-likes are total turn-offs for him kind of knocks holes in the images that movies, magazines and Madison Avenue have pounded into the minds of these young girls.

Plus, when Jim Pat says he doesn't find skinny girls attractive, they believe him. They've seen his girlfriend. Eat your heart out, Kate.

Anne Russ and Nancy Russ

CHAPTER 6

The next day started far too early. My alarm clock went off at six, and I was at the funeral home—Big Gulp in hand—by seven. The Big Gulp is how I track time. Not only does the cup get lighter, but so does the color of the liquid coming up through the straw. By the time my drink is a very pale peach rather than bright orange, I know it's about 10:30.

When I arrived, Grandpa was already there, looking chipper despite the early hour. My grandfather is a handsome man. He has a shock of white hair that pretty much does what it wants. Tall and lean, Grandpa still hasn't developed that shoulder slump that many men experience when they reach a certain age. But his eyes are what make my grandfather truly beautiful. After 90 years, his blue eyes still sparkle. One might go so far as to say they twinkle. Dad and Mo have those exact same eyes. The three men have no other common physical characteristics, but the eyes give away the family connection.

Funeral directors don't always keep such long hours, but we had agreed to meet early to go over plans for Mr. Kirby's funeral day after tomorrow. The funeral service was to be held at the Calvary Baptist Church, but the burial service would be down in South Arkansas, where Mr. Kirby wanted to be laid to rest next to his wife of 43 years. We decided that Grandpa and Mo would go with the body, and I would stay in the office and on call.

By eight we were at the Second Baptist Church for Wendell Waltham's funeral. I wasn't quite awake yet and wondered if I was up to Brother Munson's perpetually cheery disposition. He greeted us at the door.

"Brother Gibbs! Sister Gibbs! So good to see you!" he exclaimed giving us both great big bear hugs. "Cynthia and I were just saying the other day it's a shame that we only see you on such somber occasions. We've just got to have y'all out to the house for supper some night soon."

Brother Munson may like to eat as much as I do. The man refers to his rapidly expanding pot belly as "a fried chicken graveyard." I'm not making that up. His wife's recipe for chicken and dumplings is considered the best in town, so it should not surprise anyone to see that Brother Munson is beginning to look a little bit like a dumpling himself.

No matter what the occasion, the right Reverend Harvey Munson has the same smile on his face. It kind of bothers me. Perhaps I'm just cynical. Maybe his relationship with the Good Lord is so tight that nothing can shake his faith—but I don't buy it. As Winona Ryder said in the movie *Heathers*, "Nobody's happy all the time. If we were, we wouldn't be human. We'd be game show hosts." There is wisdom to be found in low-budget cinema.

Mo had already arrived and had Wendell Waltham's casket placed in the sanctuary. After Glenda had seen the yellow hue of her brother's skin, she told us to skip the make-up and opted for a closed casket. I had to wonder how many of the people who would attend this funeral today knew about Wendell's drinking problem. Brother Munson and his flock are adamantly opposed to alcohol in any size, shape or fashion. They try once about every three years to have Hilltop declared "dry", but the Methodists, Episcopalians and Catholics have a larger lobbying effort.

As the florists were setting up, I couldn't help wondering if Brother Munson knew about Wendie's problem. He had to know, didn't he? I generally don't sit in on the actual funeral service, but I decided I'd stick around on this one and see what Reverend Munson had to say about the man who drank himself to death.

The church began to fill up. Wendell Waltham had lived in this town all his life, and, despite post-mortem reports to the contrary, he was a nice guy whom everyone liked. At nine o'clock on the dot, Beulah began to sing *The Lord's Prayer*. As she belted out the final *Amen*, Reverend Munson stepped up to the podium to begin the eulogy.

"Friends, it is a sad yet joyous occasion that brings us together today. It is sad because our friend Wendell Waltham has been taken from us too soon. We all loved Wendell, and his absence will be felt for a long time. Yet, it is also a joyous occasion. As Christians, we know that the Lord sent his son, Jesus Christ, to die for all of our sins so that we might live eternally. And I tell you today that Wendell Waltham is praising the Lord in heaven as I speak.

"I believe if Wendell were here today, he would urge all of you to beware of the temptations of the secular world in which we Christians must live until it is our time to be with Jesus. Wendell would warn you because he knows the price that must be paid when one bows to temptation. He knows all too well.

"Brothers and sisters, what is your temptation? Is it liquor or drugs? Is it the lure of easy money on the riverboats? Is it the desire for another who is not your spouse? Whatever it is, turn away from it and run toward the light of the Lord. I believe Wendell would want that. For Wendell Waltham was a good man. A good man. But like all of us, he had flaws. And unfortunately, one of his was fatal.

"Before Wendell died, we had a chance to pray together, and Wendell asked the Lord's forgiveness for his sins. Praise the Lord! On this sad day, we can rejoice that even a man like Wendell, who could not remain steadfast in the face of temptation, is right this very minute fellowshipping with the Lord. Let us pray."

It was pretty tame for Brother Munson. I've known him to literally trash the deceased and intimate that the dearly departed most likely didn't make it into the Pearly Gates. Sometimes he even uses the word hell (although he pronounces it "hail"). Considering the circumstances, I thought ol' Wendie got a pretty good send off.

At the graveside service, Munson pretty much did a repeat of the church service. I noticed that Glenda seemed more agitated than mournful. I was concerned that something about our services was causing the agitation. After all the attendees had paid their respects, I approached her.

"I'm LuLu Gibbs with Gibbs Funeral Home. Is everything okay, Ms...is it still Waltham?" I asked when I realized I didn't know her last name.

"It's Justice now, but please call me Glenda," she said. "Who the hell does that man think he is!"

"What man?" I asked, hoping the answer wasn't Grandpa or Mo.

"That Reverend Munster or whatever his name is. How dare he trash my brother like that. In public! At his funeral!"

By this point, she was crying, but they were tears of rage, not grief.

"Ms. Justice...Glenda, I have a noon appointment, but I would really like a chance to talk with you about this. Could you meet me for coffee around four o'clock at The Diner?"

Not only did I want to explain to her that folks around here wouldn't see that sermon as reflecting badly on her brother, I thought this would be a great opportunity to get the scoop on where she had been for the last 30 years.

"Yes," she nodded, wiping her eyes. "I'd like that. I'll see you at four."

I had just enough time to get to the Club Car to meet Jim Pat for lunch. The Club Car is a couple of railroad cars turned into a restaurant and bar. It actually sits on a piece of track that the railroads no longer use. It's a popular lunch spot for a lot of business people in town, and it's the place to be on Saturday night. When I say "the place," I don't mean it's the best place—I mean it is the one and only place that stays open past 10 o'clock.

CHAPTER 7

Jim Pat was walking up as I pulled into the parking lot. We exchanged pecks on the cheek and went in.

One thing that hasn't changed about Jim Pat is his shyness. It took three months of my walking in the drugstore to get him to ask me out. And even then he didn't exactly ask.

"Lu, I heard that the new Wesley Snipes movie is out on video," he said. "I can't wait to see it."

Now you have to understand that the only movie theater in Hilltop shows all of three movies, so for most films, we wait for the video. You also must know that when it comes to action/adventure films, I am very much in touch with my masculine side. I love 'em.

"Oh, really," I replied, oh-so-casually. "Why don't you pick it up after work and bring it over to my place tonight?"

"Oh, gosh," he said (no kidding, the man still says "gosh" and "gee" on a regular basis). "That'd be great…if it wouldn't be too much trouble. I could bring some pizza and beer. Or soda, if you prefer."

"Either one's fine," I said. "See you around seven?"

"Okay. I'll be there."

And that was how Jim Pat Whirley asked me out on our first date. Since that is how our first date transpired, you won't be surprised to know that it took him until our fifteenth date to even get up the nerve to kiss me. We've been dating for about six months, and I figure I've got at least another nine to twelve months before sex even becomes an issue. And that's just fine with me.

I had a couple of heavy relationships during and after college—and both ended badly. What I like most about Jim Pat is that he can make chills run up and down my spine just peeking at me over the top of his menu. I'm not ready to give that up yet.

Actually, I don't know why he even opens that menu. We eat here about once a week. Every week, he pores over the same menu, and every week, he orders the exact same thing—a mushroom Swiss burger with sweet potato fries. This week was no different. I find the whole ritual extremely comforting.

"So what's up?" I asked.

"Mom's on a tirade again over Uncle Whit's divorce," he lamented. "She keeps talking about how I'm being robbed of my birthright."

As I mentioned before, Whit Whitney runs the family bank, and he also owns both dry cleaners and several coin-operated washaterias in town. The man has money running out of his ears, and his soon-to-be ex-wife is putting him through the wringer (no pun intended).

"I still can't believe Uncle Whit got involved with that woman," Jim Pat said. "How could he do that to Aunt Carlene?"

Mr. Whitney is definitely the victim of a violent mid-life crisis. Apparently, something completely snapped in his brain and caused him to go chasing after a bank teller half his age. Word is he'd been sleeping with this particular employee for over a year when he finally announced to his wife that he was leaving. He figured they'd get a quiet divorce; he'd make sure Carlene was comfortable for the rest of her life, and then in about a year, he would marry 25-five-year-old Tiffany and live happily ever after.

Boy did he miscalculate! Not only did Mrs. Whitney know about the affair for some time—she had pictures! So as you can imagine, she's going for the jugular. Which, in the case of Whit Whitney, is located in his wallet.

I know most of the story from what Jim Pat has told me, but some of it comes from Reverend Thad. He's been very distressed over the entire situation. The Whitneys are members of his congregation, and Mr. Whitney serves on the board of deacons. Thad feels that in light of what has happened, Mr. Whitney ought to step down, but the little cradle robber refuses. It would take a vote of the deacons to recommend his removal; and since all the deacons do business at his bank, that seems highly unlikely. Yes, Thad finds the whole situation extremely distressing.

Now don't be thinking badly about Brother Toomey for telling me about congregational troubles. Even a minister needs a counselor from time to time, and as a licensed social worker, I'm about as close as you'll come in Hilltop.

"Since Aunt Carlene and Uncle Whit live in the old family home, she's trying to lay claim to the house and everything in it," Jim Pat continued. "A lot of that stuff has been in the family for generations. Since they don't have any kids, I'm the sole Whitney heir. I don't really care all that much about the stuff, but Mom keeps crying about how her grandchildren will be robbed of their heritage all because her brother had a major case of mid life crazies."

"So, then, you're looking forward to the big family Thanksgiving dinner?" I asked, attempting to lighten the mood.

Jim Pat grinned. He doesn't smile—he grins. If you don't understand the difference, I can't explain it to you.

Right then our food arrived. Jim Pat's usual and a big Club Car salad for me. It's the house specialty. It's everything you would put on a club sandwich—ham, turkey, bacon, cheese, tomatoes and lettuce—all put in a big bowl rather than between pieces of bread. They also have this secret recipe house dressing that is to die for. I've tried experimenting at home to figure out the ingredients, but so far, I've failed miserably.

"So what's up with you?" he asked. "Was the funeral fun?"

He asks the same question about every funeral, and he always phrases the question just that way. He claims there is no appropriate way to inquire about a funeral, so it's easier just to be inappropriate.

He's right about that one. What are you supposed to say when, on your return from the funeral of a loved one, someone asks, "How was the funeral?"

Don't you just want to scream "It was really, really sad, you moron! Someone died. How do you think it was?"

I told him about Reverend Munson's sermon and about my coffee date with the sister of the deceased.

"Oh, I remember those stories about her," Jim Pat recalled. "Didn't she run off with the carnival and become some sort of side-show attraction—bearded lady or something?"

"It was the circus, and she was a contortionist," I said, jogging his memory. "I found out she left the circus three years after she left Hilltop. I'm going to find out this afternoon what happened during the rest of the last 30 years."

"Miss Mattie will be so relieved," he said.

"Why?" I asked, thinking he knew something I didn't know.

"Because, contrary to popular opinion, she can't live forever. I think she'll just rest easier knowing that when her time comes, you'll be there ready to take up the torch of the town gossip."

The crouton I threw hit him right on the nose.

31

Anne Russ and Nancy Russ

CHAPTER 8

After Jim Pat and I parted company, I headed back to the office. I still had about two-and-a-half hours before I was to meet Hilltop's prodigal daughter for coffee, and I decided to use that time to update our cards.

In the funeral business, you have to be very careful about the way you market and advertise your product. You can't be too splashy and offer up a whimsical, eye-catching message. "We put the 'fun' back in 'funerals'" just doesn't cut it. Nor do you want to be too stuffy with your message, or you can end up looking positively morbid. Because Gibbs is the only game in town, we don't have to do too much in the way of promotions, but we like to keep a good image within the community.

Gibbs Funeral home has our own co-ed junior softball league in the summer, and we team up with the local American Cancer Society Chapter to do a memorial tree of lights at Christmas time.

But our biggest PR effort is our cards. We send condolence cards commemorating the anniversary of our clients' deaths. This may sound a bit odd, but of all the services Gibbs offers, our condolence cards are the most appreciated. Many people don't realize how long the grieving process takes. Right after a death, those left behind are often too busy to grieve. There are decisions to make regarding the funeral, personal effects, the estate, etc. There is also a constant barrage of people wanting to know what they can do to help—an around the clock support system. But eventually, people have to go back to their own lives, and they assume that the bereaved will go on with theirs.

Very often the worst experience of grief comes later. In fact, grief can sort of sneak up on people. They're waltzing through life, thinking that everything is fine and then that first anniversary comes and hits them right between the eyes. For some people, that first anniversary can be every bit as traumatic as the death, and the grieving find themselves without the support system they had the year before.

Because of this, Gibbs Funeral home always sends a card to the family members on the anniversary of their loved one's death. It doesn't sound like much, but it's amazing how much the family appreciates the fact that someone else remembers their loss. We send cards every year for at least five years—sometimes longer. Grandpa used to just use a big wall calendar to keep track, but I have the whole system computerized now. Every week, the anniversaries for the next week pop up on my screen. I prepare the cards, but Grandpa adds a personal note and signs every card that goes out.

People appreciate these remembrances so much that at Christmas time, we get besieged with homemade goodies—fudge, brownies, divinity, cookies—you name it, it's here. One year, it got so out of hand that we held an open house at Dad and Grandpa's just so the food wouldn't go to waste. It's a wonderful problem to have.

In addition to the cards, the family also receives a letter about our grief seminars. We hold six to eight week sessions three or four times a year. The upcoming pre-holiday sessions are always the best attended. The first big holiday celebration from which a family member is absent is always a doozy for the grieving.

By the time I wrapped up the cards and correspondence for this week and left them on Grandpa's desk, it was time to meet Glenda at The Diner. She was waiting at a corner booth when I arrived. I sat down, and Trish, who has been a fixture at The Diner for as long as anyone can remember, came and took our coffee orders. I also ordered a slice of cherry pie. The Diner has the best pies west of the Mississippi. If you don't have your Thanksgiving order in by early November, you're out of luck.

When I was a little girl, The Diner even made the national news wires. Sometime in the 70s the Smiths (no relation to the other Mrs. Smith of pie fame) who had owned The Diner for years sold the business to Bo and Ruth Thompson. Problem was the Thompsons assumed that the pie recipes came with the business. The Diner is a full service restaurant, but they make their money on pies like some places do on beer and liquor.

The Smiths (they were Mrs. Smith's recipes) refused to turn over the recipes, saying that wasn't part of the contract and nobody else was going to make their pies. So the new owners actually took the former owners to court over pie recipes. If Court TV had been around then, the case would have been broadcast from coast to coast. As it was, the story made the AP newswires and was printed around the country. In the end, the Thompsons dropped the suit after their lawyer discovered that the recipes weren't written down anywhere—they were all in Mrs. Smith's head—all 13 recipes. The lawyer told them even if they won, there was no way to force the Smiths to give them the exact recipes. So the Thompsons learned to make their own pies, which weren't bad; but they were not the same.

About five years later, when Mrs. Smith passed away (two months after Mr. Smith died), she left those recipes on handwritten cards willed to the Thompsons. Said they were just too good to take with her to the grave.

As I related the story to Glenda, she let out a really long rich laugh like someone who wasn't afraid or ashamed to revel in a little tale of small-town life or draw a little attention to herself. In contrast to the severe suit she had worn to the funeral, Glenda was now wearing loose fitting fawn colored slacks and a sage green twin sweater set. She looked the most relaxed and at ease I had seen her since she made her re-entrance into Hilltop.

"Thank you so much for meeting me," she said. "I'm actually feeling a bit better. Reverend Munson came up and spoke to me after the service. It turns out he really did think quite a lot of Wendell. He actually apologized to me."

"For what he said in the service?" I asked, thinking that would be very unlike Brother Munson.

"No," she said. "I think you were right about that. He thought he was being very kind. No, he apologized to me for not knowing that Wendie had a problem until it was too late. He said as Wendie's minister, it was his job to know when his members were struggling, and he should have done something to help. He's actually quite torn up about it. I know how he feels. I had no idea Wendie had gotten in such bad shape. If I had been around more, I might have been able to do something."

While I used my best soothing voice to reassure Glenda that she wasn't to blame for her brother's death, I breathed an inward sigh of relief. Funerals are hard enough without having a controversial sub-plot enter into the picture. I thought Glenda's earlier grievance had been justified, but you'd be amazed at some of the things people can get bent out of shape over at a funeral.

The biggest debacle I've encountered thus far was two sisters who were burying their father. When it was time to get in the limo and go from the church to the cemetery, the eldest sister refused to get in the car with her younger sibling. It seems baby sister was "living in sin" with a man she had neglected to marry, and big sister decided that riding in the same car with the partners on the way to Daddy's funeral would somehow be condoning the arrangement. The thing that really got me about that is that the eldest sibling failed to mention her righteous indignation until the moment it was time to get into the car. Hello! Gibbs does own two limos and could have arranged for both. We can even borrow a third from the funeral home in the next town if need be. As it was, big sis got to ride with me in the Honda and little sis and her significant other had an opportunity to contemplate their evil ways during a luxury ride to the cemetery.

"Well, I'm glad you're feeling better about the service," I told Glenda. "In spite of the circumstances, are you glad to be back in Hilltop?"

"I didn't think I would be, but it is nice to be back home," she said. "You're too young to remember, but I'm sure you've heard the story about my running off with the circus."

I nodded, but didn't say anything.

"I stayed with them for about three years, and at the time, I was far too embarrassed to come home. Then, as the years went by, it just seemed kind of silly to come back. I severed ties with everyone here—except Wendell—and it seemed a little rude just to pop back into their lives after all this time."

Trish brought our coffee and my pie. It just looked too tempting. Glenda ordered a slice as well. This is the one issue I've found where I differ from my TV-buddy Rosie. She doesn't like fruit in her dessert. How can anyone not like fruit? Maybe you have to grow up in Arkansas to know how great the first watermelon of the summer tastes or exactly when you can count on the fresh peaches to show up at the roadside produce stands. And then, when you can combine fruit and pastry to bring about that wonderful creation known as pie, there's just not much that's better. Someday Rosie and I may have to chat about this. She obviously has just not met the right pie.

"So," I asked casually, wiping a crumb from the corner of my mouth. "What have you been doing all these years?"

"Oh, this and that," she answered evasively. "I did eventually marry, but my husband passed away a year ago, and I've been trying to decide what to do next."

"Are you planning to stay in Hilltop much longer?" I asked, trying a different tactic.

"You know, I wasn't planning to, but it really has felt good to be back. No one seems to care that I vanished without a trace 30 years ago. Everyone has been so nice. Wendell's house is mine now, and I've always had a flair for design. It breaks my heart to see how the house has run down. And the yard has really been neglected. I remember when that house and its gardens were the show place of the county. I may just stay around and fix up the old place."

OK, so I hadn't unearthed any deep, dark secrets, but I did find out that the mysterious Glenda had been married, likes to garden and perhaps at one time had done some interior decorating. I know it's not much, but it will satisfy my curiosity until I can uncover more info.

By this time we had each consumed three cups of coffee from Trish's bottomless pot, and when the bill came Glenda reached for it.

"Nothing doing," I said. "I invited you. And besides, I think Gibbs can spring for a 75 cent cup of coffee and a piece of pie."

"Thank you. I've really enjoyed this."

I handed her my card. "If you do decide to stay, please give me a call. I know things move slowly around here, but I'm sure there have been some changes over the last 30 years. If you need help with anything at all, please let me know."

We walked out of the shop together, and Glenda got into a late-model beige Mercedes SE. So, there were some bucks somewhere. Also, the car had a Florida license tag. I was slowly accumulating more pieces to the Glenda Justice puzzle. Miss Mattie would be proud.

Anne Russ and Nancy Russ

CHAPTER 9

Mr. Kirby's funeral went as well as funerals can go. Molly was no longer hysterical. She had known that her father was not long for this world, but I think she expected another stroke and perhaps a short stint in the hospital during which time she could prepare herself and say goodbye.

"I never got a chance to say good-bye."

I hear that every week. Nobody wants someone they love to suffer a horrible illness, but everyone who loses someone suddenly wishes they had a warning so they could say a final goodbye.

But the thing that tears my heart apart every time I hear it is, "I never got the chance to say 'I love you.'"

I have learned how not to cry at funerals we do, but that one brings tears to my eyes every time. Being in constant contact with death makes you very aware of the precariousness of life. My family never lets a day go by without telling each other how we feel. I say "good-night" and "I love you" to Dad and Grandpa every day, and they do the same to me. Jim Pat and I aren't to the "I love you" stage just yet, but I know that if either of us died tomorrow, he would know how very much I cared about him.

Fortunately Molly's father knew how much she loved him, and she knew that he knew. It may not seem like such a big deal on a day to day basis, but it's huge once someone is gone.

That was one of the reasons Thad held up so well at this funeral.

"You know, Lu," he told me earlier, "I can deal with the ones that aren't so tragic. I know Molly's gonna miss her dad, but she had a lot of years with him, and she really values that. She will grieve, but she will be okay."

"Is it easier when the deceased is older?" I asked, trying to get a handle on what touched this sensitive man so deeply.

"Not necessarily. For me, anyway. Remember when Mr. Baker died last year?

I remembered.

"I didn't know the man that well, but apparently he had a huge need to be in control of everything around him. His three sons got tired of being badgered and left town years ago. I think the youngest said he called at Christmas, but that was the only contact any of them had with him for years. Mr. Baxter died alone and guilt-ridden over the way he treated his kids, and the sons arrived for the funeral feeling equally guilty. They mourned the years they had missed with their father."

"Didn't you come down with a bad stomach flu right after that?"

Thad smiled a little as he turned to go to the pulpit, "Lu, I've never had flu in my life, but it doesn't look too good for a minister to be too sad to get out of bed."

Thad talked about Mr. Kirby's life and how he had made the most of the time he had here. An old army buddy had driven all the way from Texas to tell the congregation how Mr. Kirby's bravery and selflessness had saved his life 50 years before. It was my favorite kind of funeral—a celebration of a life.

As planned, Mo and Grandpa took the body down to South Arkansas for the graveside service. I went back to the office to be on call and catch up on some reading.

I love our building. Because of the nature of the business, funeral homes give a lot of people the creeps, but ours is designed to make people feel as comfortable as possible. There is a small lobby at the entrance that leads into a chapel. Grandpa designed the chapel himself. Instead of dark wood, all the pews and the altar are light oak. The cathedral style windows are clear so that light shines through during the day. The carpets and cushions are a deep royal blue. The idea is to have a light, airy place for services. Grandpa says people are depressed enough when they attend a funeral; they shouldn't have to sit in a depressing room. The chapel can comfortably seat 150, but our record is 225—with a lot of people spilling out into the lobby.

Even though most folks in Hilltop belong to one church or another, we hold quite a few memorial services in our chapel. A lot of people don't want the place where they worship on Sunday to be the place where they say good-bye to someone they love. One woman said she just knew that every Sunday morning, instead of seeing the reverend and the choir up at the front of the church, all she'd be able to see was her husband's coffin covered in flowers. Still other folks wouldn't hold a funeral anywhere but a church. Death is a sacred thing, and for some, the funeral home chapel just isn't holy ground.

The room to the left of the foyer is the display room. We stock 15 different caskets, but we can special order just about anything. I was surprised by how seriously people take the casket decision. I mean, it's going into the ground, and the person who died isn't going to actually need to be comfortable in it. But people who are preplanning can be very specific about their casket choices and people who are picking caskets for a deceased loved one can get into knock-down, drag-out fights about which one to choose. Mo literally had to come in and break up a fight between two brothers who were fighting over whether their mother would have an oak or a mahogany casket. I finally had to make a special order for an oak casket with a mahogany inlay just so we could go ahead and bury the poor woman.

Some folks do handle their disputes better than those boys. About six months ago, Hettie Sue, who had run the local post office for as long as I had been living, died. She had four grown kids and all of them showed up to plan the funeral. Everything was going just fine until time to choose the casket. I had already pegged the youngest sister, Darla, as a bit of a drama queen. I know she was grieving, but she carried this little lacy handkerchief that she kept dabbing her eyes with (even though they were dry). As I was explaining the planning process to them, she let out a loud wail every time I paused to see if there were questions.

So when we got to the casket selection, the other three just asked which was the least expensive.

Darla let out another wail and said, "You cannot bury my mama in a cheap casket. We want this one."

She picked out our deluxe and most pricey model. The two brothers just kind of looked helpless. I knew that none of them had tons of money, but I'm sure they also didn't want to feel like misers when it came to their own mother. Big Sis took a different approach.

"Look, Darla," she said. "If you believe half of what they spout at that church where you seem to be every time they open the doors, you know that Mama has departed that body and isn't going to care what kind of casket we put it in. But if it's so important to you, then the boys and I will split the cost of this casket, and you can make up the difference and get whatever one you want."

I've never seen anybody back pedal so fast. Yep, our casket room has seen a lot of action.

41

Mo keeps a little office off the side of the preparation room in back. He has a small desk and a little filing cabinet where he keeps all the records of how the deceased came to us and where we bury them. Grandpa has offered him more space several times, but Mo insists that he has all he needs to do his job.

Grandpa's office is off to the left. This is where we conduct most of our funeral planning. In addition to a big oak desk, there is also a round conference table in the center of the room where we generally meet with families.

My office is next to Grandpa's, and I love it. My desk and computer sit against the far wall beneath a window that looks out over the lawn. The room is dominated by a fluffy couch and two big chairs that swallow you up when you sit down. These three pieces surround an overstuffed ottoman. I've always felt that furniture that allows you nowhere to prop your feet is simply not functional.

My office is kind of the unofficial calming den for Gibbs Funeral Home. Often during a visitation, a planning or even a service, one member of the family gets completely overwrought and needs a place to take a time-out from the proceedings. Sitting in one of my chairs with feet up and a hot cup of tea in hand has worked wonders for many a mourner.

I spent the remainder of the afternoon in one of those chairs, reading the latest book by Earl Grollman. It may sound like a leisurely afternoon to most, but I try to read at least a book a week relating to death and dying, grief counseling or funeral planning. As in any other profession, you have to keep up with the latest information.

The foreword in this book was a quote from Abraham Lincoln who lost three sons:

> In this sad world of ours, sorrow comes to all…
> It comes with bitterest agony…
> Perfect relief is not possible, except with time…
> You cannot now realize that you will ever feel better…
> And yet, this is a mistake.
> You are sure to be happy again.
> To know this, which is certainly true,
> Will make you come less miserable now.
> I have experienced enough to know what I say.

CHAPTER 10

What I thought was going to be a lazy Saturday turned into a rather interesting day. It was cool and crisp outside—light jacket weather. The leaves had turned but not all of them had fallen, so the ground and the trees were awash with shades of greens, golds and reds. I was planning to spend some time in the hammock that hangs in the yard between my little place and the main house. But it was not to be.

Mo got the call from Doc Green that Mrs. Street had passed away at Hilltop Manor, our upscale assisted living facility. Generally, on such an occasion, Mo would bring the body to our place and either Grandpa or I would meet with the family on Monday morning or afternoon. However, Mrs. Street's daughters were all in town and wanted to meet about the funeral as soon as possible.

"How can they all be in town?" I asked Mo. "Joan is the only one who lives here. How did Janice and Julia get here so quickly?"

"Actually, Mrs. Street passed away last night about 10 o'clock. I got the call and went to get the body. I didn't see any reason to call you at the time. Apparently, she rang the call button in her room, and when the orderly arrived he found her not breathing. The hospital notified the family right away. Julia caught a red-eye and Janice drove in from St. Louis. So they're all here and they want to meet—today."

I could tell Mo was tense. As I mentioned before, dealing with the living is not his forte.

"Well, I haven't even showered yet, but I think I can be there in an hour," I said reluctantly. "Will that do?"

"Yes, I'll let them know."

When I finished with a quick shower, I perused my closet trying to decide which pantsuit to wear. That's all I ever wear to work—pantsuits. I haven't worn a pair of panty hose since my high school graduation, and I simply cannot endure those high-heeled pumps that were so obviously invented by a man. So the pantsuit is my unofficial uniform. I think I have over 25 now. Most of them, of course, are in subdued colors—black, navy, taupe, forest green. I do own a fabulous red suit and an emerald green one that looks smashing with my hair.

Today I opted for a pale blue double breasted number that is rather casual, but nice enough for an impromptu funeral planning.

I grew up with Joan's daughter, Margaret, and I knew the whole family. Mrs. Street had been ill for several months. Her daughters had begged her to hire some live-in help, but she didn't want "strangers" in her home. She also refused to move in with Joan because she didn't want "to be a burden" to her children. Eventually she had to take up residence at Hilltop Manor. After the move, she only got worse.

When I arrived at the funeral home, Margaret and all three of Mrs. Street's daughters were waiting. I hugged Margaret and asked the cause of death.

"Doc Green says officially it was heart failure," she said. "But he said there was no real reason for her heart to give out. I guess she just decided it was time to die."

I shook hands with Joan, Janice and Julia. I didn't know any of them very well. Margaret's mother Joan is the oldest. She's an attractive lady. The kind of Southern woman who always looks impeccable, but doesn't look like she's made much of an effort to look that way. She wears her dark hair in a short pageboy. It is starting to gray, and she doesn't try to camouflage it. Her nails are perfectly manicured but unpolished. Her clothes are simple, but tasteful and well-fitting. She always volunteered for things when Margaret and I were in school. She makes the best cupcakes. The other mothers only made simple chocolate or white cupcakes, but Joan used to make fancy ones like carrot cake or cheesecake.

Janice, the youngest, looked as if she might fall apart any minute. Everything about her looks soft. She has that kind of rounded, supple figure that so many women develop when they reach their mid-fifties or so—not fat, just soft. And her skin has a creamy texture that looks almost velvety. Even in her distressed state, you could tell she's the kind of person who is generally offering comfort to others. From Margaret, I knew she became a school music teacher and church organist.

Mrs. Street visited Janice often in St. Louis, and the two of them always went on a trip for several weeks each summer. In addition to Paris, Rome and London, they went to exotic places like Morocco, Kenya, India and China. Mrs. Street's home is a showcase of all the places she and her daughter have been. I've only been in it two or three times, but it's really beautiful.

Janice never married and always spent her holidays here in Hilltop. Occasionally, I'd see her and her mother around town, and they really seemed to enjoy each other—more like best friends than mother and daughter.

Julia is another story. She has traveled all over the world as well, but with her husband who was a career Navy man. I think Margaret told me he is retired now, and they live somewhere on the coast of Virginia. She is painfully thin. And I mean it pains me to look at her and think about how little food she must take in to be that skinny. With her pinched face and her undernourished body, she is a stark contrast to Janice. I got the impression that Julia is not close to the rest of the family.

I ushered the three women into Grandpa's office and we all settled around the conference table.

"Now, where will the funeral be held?" I began.

"At Calvary Baptist," Julia spoke right up.

Janice, who looked exhausted, corrected her.

"No," she said. "Mother wants the funeral to be at the church in Pilgrim's Rest where she grew up."

Pilgrim's Rest is a little community right outside of town that has an interesting history. It got its name from the cemetery. The story is that during the depression, a family from Oklahoma was passing through Arkansas in a covered wagon when one of their six children died. They stopped and buried the child in a field. (No one is quite sure now whether it was a boy or girl.) The people in the community didn't have much to give to the family, but they made a stone slab to cover the top of the grave, and carved the word "Pilgrim" on it. Obviously, the field could no longer be used for anything else, so the owners turned it into the "Pilgrim's Rest Cemetery," and the name stuck for the community. The little church there is Primitive Baptist and has about 40 members. They have four men who rotate the preaching duty every month. I don't think they even draw a salary.

"That's ridiculous!" Julia said, in a surprisingly loud voice. "Mother has been a member at Calvary Baptist Church for nearly 50 years. It's been a huge part of her life."

"We know," Janice said. "But mother told Joan and me exactly what she wanted when she moved into Hilltop Manor, and we promised to carry out her wishes."

"She never told me that," Julia said emphatically.

This time Joan spoke.

"She might have, if you had been around," she said softly.

Julia ignored her.

"Good heavens," she lamented. "I don't think that falling down little church even has an organ."

"It doesn't," answered Janice patiently. "Mother wants cousin Blake to play his bagpipes and the Pilgrim Run Boys to sing."

The Pilgrim Run Boys are a local quartet who have been singing together for about 40 years. Individually, none of them has a very stellar singing voice, but something amazing happens when they come together. I've heard them at different town and county events over the years, but I have to say, I've never heard them at a funeral.

An exasperated Julia turned to Joan.

"Are you going to let her do this?"

"I most certainly am," Joan said. "Mother planned everything, right down to the music and flowers. We are going to respect her wishes."

Julia glared at both of them but offered no further objections.

When the three daughters went to look at coffins, Margaret whispered to me, "Aunt Julia has hardly spoken to Gram for the last ten years, but just watch—at the funeral she'll be the one who cries the loudest and longest."

The rest of the arrangements were made without any further conflict. The obituary would appear in Sunday's paper and the service would be held on Monday. Mrs. Street had requested that Grandpa not only direct the service but also conduct it. I found that a little surprising. We had never been close friends with Mrs. Street. However, I knew Grandpa would agree to do it if that was what the family wanted.

CHAPTER 11

Sunday was lunch at Uncle Billy's and Aunt Letitia's. Dad, Grandpa and I rode over together. We all live in the same house—sort of. When Mom left, Dad and I moved into the large, Victorian-style house where he grew up. He said he just couldn't stay in the home he and Mom had built and decorated together.

When we moved in, Grandpa moved out back to the guesthouse. He claimed he didn't want to fool with the upkeep of the big house, and he was too set in his ways to live with other people again (Grandma had passed away before I was born). When I came back to Hilltop three years ago, Grandpa decided to move back into the big house with Dad. He said at his age, you needed to have someone else in the house. He's always talking about how things are "at his age". And since very few people make it to that age, there aren't many around to dispute his claims.

So I moved into the guesthouse. It's really quite nice. There's a full kitchen, a living area, a large bedroom and a bath. Because the rent is so cheap (zilch), I could afford to do a little remodeling when I moved in. With the help of cousin Frank, I expanded the bathroom to include a whirlpool bath and a separate shower that converts into a steam room as well. Yes, it is a little extravagant—especially for Hilltop—but I chalk it up to the cost of maintaining my sanity. I don't drink, smoke or take any drugs stronger than an antihistamine in the spring; but I have been known to disappear into my oasis of a bathroom for hours at a time. Citrus scented oils and soaps are my favorite.

As we pulled up to my aunt and uncle's large colonial home, I noted their newly-painted red front door. On their last vacation to the New England area, Letitia fell in love with the traditional red door that adorns many of the homes there. She and Billy had been arguing back and forth about it for several months, and apparently she had won. Instead of looking out of place, as I thought it might, the door actually looked quite stylish and inviting. I told her just that as she opened the door.

"Oh, Lu! Aren't you sweet?" she gushed. "I do think it looks *tres chic*, but Billy is still adjusting. The girls in the Magnolia Club just adore it."

Letitia never misses an opportunity to remind you that she is a member of the book club that claims to be the "oldest book club west of the Mississippi." Now how anyone could actually dispute or prove that, I have no idea. The average age of the "girls" in the club is about 65. Long before Oprah was even born, the Magnolia Club was gathering to discuss the latest literary masterpieces and/or best sellers.

You must be invited to join the Magnolia Club, and everyone in the club must vote to accept you. If one person doesn't want you, you're out. There are 18, and *only 18,* members of the club. They meet nine months of the year and take summers off. The schedule rotates so that each year nine members host a meeting at their home, and the other nine each review a book; so each member reviews one year and hosts the next. Letitia likes entertaining far more than she likes reading, and some of the members enjoy doing reviews. So, when it's Lettie's turn to review, she swaps with someone who is scheduled to host. I doubt Aunt Lettie has read any of the books reviewed in her six years of membership.

Today Aunt Lettie looked impeccable in a short-sleeved, little black dress cinched at the waist with a bright red belt (to match the door, perhaps?). Her hair—just the right shade of ash blonde—was swept back in a chignon, and not a strand was out of place. Letitia doesn't look any younger than her 48 years, but she does look like a woman who has aged well—very well.

"Y'all come in and have a seat. Dinner will be ready *toute suite!*"

I could feel Grandpa wincing behind me every time a French phrase came out of Aunt Lettie's mouth. He thinks anyone who chooses to speak in a foreign language when no foreigners are present is simply putting on airs. He probably has a point; but as I mentioned before, Letitia's cooking is definitely worth enduring a little pretension.

We sat down, and Uncle Billy said to my Dad, "So, Bobby, I hear there may be some trouble down at the bank."

Grandpa and I both looked at Dad. Dad doesn't like to talk about things he doesn't enjoy; therefore Grandpa and I never hear about what's going on at the bank. What we do hear about is what kind of fish are biting at the local pond and what type of flora is the latest addition to the Garden of Eden Dad has created in the back yard.

"Looks like there might be," Dad said. "Whit really stepped in it this time."

Dad stopped to take a drink of the iced tea Aunt Lettie had handed him.

"Apparently Whit's had several offers from the big banks to buy him out. He and Nancy won't hear of it; they want to keep the bank a community run bank like it's always been. Since they control 56 percent of the voting stock, nobody else on the board can do anything about it. There are a couple of people who would make a killing on some of the deals the bank has been offered, and they resent the hell out of the fact that Whit and Nancy won't sell."

Dad paused to take another sip of tea.

"This is right good tea, Lettie," he commented. "Do I detect a hint of mint?"

Before Lettie could answer, I interrupted.

"Dad, the bank?"

Dad is easily distracted and often has to be steered back on course.

"Oh, yes," he continued. "Well, you all know that Carlene Whitney is madder than a wet hen about her husband stepping out on her and all. And who could blame her? This is a small town and she feels completely humiliated. I don't know what upsets her more—that Whit cheated on her or that everybody knows about it.

"Anyway, she's going after half of his voting shares in the bank. If she gets them, she could swing the vote to sell, and we'd get gobbled up by one of those mega banks."

Grandpa said, "I thought Whit and Carlene had a prenuptial agreement."

I don't know how he knew that, but I was not surprised. Grandpa often possesses unexpected tidbits of information.

"They do. Or rather, they did," said Dad. "The whole thing is null and void if there is proof of adultery. They say Whit had that clause put in there so he wouldn't have to fork over any dough if she started fooling around. Now, I'm not a highly educated man, but I do believe that's what they call irony."

"Boy, does Carlene Whitney have proof—in living color," Uncle Billy piped up. "Ray over at the paper said she brought pictures to the

49

editorial desk and wanted *The Journal* to run them in Sunday's edition with a lengthy expose on Whit and Tiffany's relationship. That woman is about two steps away from a total breakdown."

Uncle Billy is the quintessential aging frat boy. He has the round face and body that come with too many years of rich food and drink. Even though I doubt he could run to the end of the block, he exudes a healthy vitality. I don't believe the man owns a stitch of clothing that is not a designer label. Today he was sporting highly starched khaki pants, an equally starched Ralph Lauren dark blue denim shirt and Cole Hahn tasseled loafers that were the exact shade of rich brown leather as his belt. He's the kind of man who buys his socks and underwear at an upscale department store. The only thing that is off about Uncle Billy's "look" is his lack of a tan. Most men of his ilk are involved in some outdoor activity, such as golf or tennis, that provides them with year-round color on their face and arms. But Billy's skin tone comes dangerously close to rivaling that of the Pillsbury dough boy—he hates the outdoors. He'll never have to worry about skin cancer.

Dad is his brother's physical opposite. He's almost lean enough to be officially skinny. I have no idea how I can be related to this man who forgets to eat. Honestly, if someone doesn't remind him or physically put some food before him, there's no telling how long he could go without nourishment. Regular fishing trips and working in his prized yard give Dad a permanent sun kissed (if not wind burned) glow. As far as fashion sense, well, let me just say that he still owns and wears a brown suit. I really can't talk about it.

CHAPTER 12

Grandpa had been unusually quiet all through lunch. I wondered if the death of an old friend was the reason. On the way home I asked him about it.

"Grandpa, I know you knew Mrs. Street, but I didn't realize the two of you were so close," I said. "I was surprised when I found she had asked that you conduct the service—not that you don't do a great funeral."

"Oh, yes," he said. "In another lifetime, Hester Street—Hester Allen back then—and I were sweet on each other. She was a beauty. I hate to sound like some old relic, but women just don't look that way anymore—so elegant, so graceful. She was something else."

He stopped and stared out the window.

"When the crash came, I was 21 and already working at the funeral home with my father. Times were tough; people couldn't afford to pay the funeral home; but folks kept on dying. For almost three years, we buried everyone on trade or credit. Because money was so tight, the family decided I should leave for awhile to get work. I headed out east to work on one of the bridges being built by FDR's New Deal program. I sent money back home every week for a year. Don't know that Gibbs Funeral home would be here today if it weren't for that bridge."

We pulled into the driveway. Grandpa got out and headed for the house. Dad and I were right on his heels waiting to hear the rest of this story.

"Hester and I wrote to each other all year long," Grandpa continued, sitting down in the kitchen. "On the bus ride home, all I could think about was seeing her. I was going make her my wife—if she'd have me. She was waiting for me at the bus station. She gave me a hug and a kiss, but I could tell something was wrong. We went for a walk, and she told me she was going to marry Donald Street the following week. She was carrying his child."

I couldn't believe it. Sweet little Mrs. Street? A shotgun bride?

"Looking back, I could see how the tone of her letters had changed over the year. At first she wrote about how much she missed me and what it would be like when I came home, but the later letters were really just about what was going on in town. As hurt as I was, I just couldn't blame her. Hester was already 20, and in the eyes of the world back then, it wouldn't be long before she was past her prime in terms of finding a husband. I had never promised her anything or even mentioned marriage.

"Donald Street was a good man. She said she loved him, and he loved her. About a month after their wedding, I met your grandmother. As much as losing Hester Allen hurt, missing out on the 40 years I got to spend with your grandma would have been a far more tragic fate. I guess God knows what He's doing even if He doesn't always let us in on it."

As I was absorbing this, I noticed that Dad's face sported the same stunned expression I imagined mine wore. He had never heard this story either. I guess Grandpa had not wanted to soil the good name of the first woman he ever loved.

But a thought occurred to me.

"That means Joan is almost 70," I said. "She certainly doesn't look it."

"No," said Grandpa. "She's not. Hester had a miscarriage late in the pregnancy. She almost died. All the doctors said she'd never have another child. Hester never did like being told what she could or couldn't do. I'm surprised she didn't have 10 kids just to prove those people wrong."

"Her husband has been gone almost as long as Mom has," Dad said. "Did you ever think about starting up where you left off years ago?"

Dad rarely pries for personal information—even from family—so his question surprised me a little.

"No," said Grandpa. "That was another lifetime. We were just kids. We've both gone through a life's worth of changes. Anything now just wouldn't be the same as it was then."

"Well, that's enough revelation for me for one day," I said. "Do you need me to come help set up the visitation?"

"No," Grandpa shook his head. "I'll be fine. I'd like to go a little early and have a little time by myself to say goodbye."

CHAPTER 13

I slept in a little on Monday morning. Grandpa and Mo were taking care of all the funeral arrangements, but I was going to be an attendee at this funeral. I was going to go anyway for Margaret—and to hear the Pilgrim's Run Boys. But now that I knew all about the Grandpa/Mrs. Street connection, I couldn't wait to hear what my grandfather was going to say.

It was a beautiful sunny day. Pretty weather always makes a funeral a little easier.

I met Grandpa in a room adjacent to the little sanctuary where the family had gathered. Margaret had been right on the money. Julia was sobbing hysterically. It was obvious Joan had realized that this was coming. She saw her mother every day and witnessed her declining health. She looked sad, but resigned. Janice, on the other hand, had that stunned look about her, as if it had only recently occurred to her that her mother was not going to live forever. I know that look well; I see it a lot.

Cousin Blake started the service with a rousing bagpipes rendition of *Amazing Grace*. Blake is a music teacher over at Lyon College in Batesville. It's a small liberal arts school with a strong Scottish Presbyterian tradition. I suppose it's one of the few schools in the country that has its own bagpipe ensemble. Blake directs the bagpipers and is considered one of the best players around today. Lord knows I couldn't dispute that claim, having no one to really compare him to.

After the bagpipes faded, the Pilgrim's Run Boys continued the rather un-funeral-like music by singing *This World is not My Home* to the accompaniment of a guitar and a banjo.

> This world is not my home. I'm just a passin' through
> My treasures are laid up somewhere beyond the blue
> The angels beckon me from heaven's open door
> And I can't feel at home in this world anymore.

Oh Lord you know I have no friend like you
If heaven's not my home then Lord what will I do
The angels beckoned me from heaven's open door
And I can't feel at home in this world anymore.

When "the boys" (who are actually past-middle-aged men) had finished, Grandpa took his place at the podium. He began with a verse from Proverbs:

"'How difficult it is to find a virtuous woman. She is worth far more than jewels!' Mrs. Hester Allen Street was indeed such a woman. I daresay I've known Hester longer than anyone sitting in this room here today. And I feel confident in saying that she touched each of your lives deeply.

"As a girl, Hester used to sing in the choir at this very church. I bet many of you didn't know that Hester Allen Street had a voice so sweet the angels in heaven used to turn green with envy when she wrapped it around a hymn of praise to the Lord she loved so dearly.

"As a wife, Hester was committed to her husband, Donald, for over 55 years. Theirs was the kind of marriage any couple today would do well to emulate—full of love, passion, loyalty and mutual respect.

"As a mother, Hester raised three strong, intelligent, talented daughters who have, like Hester, made the world a better place in which to be.

"As a teacher, Hester taught at least five generations of Hilltop young people the stories and lessons of the Bible.

"As a woman, Hester was a strong contributor in both human and financial resources to her church and its ministry, a faithful friend to many and a role model to all who knew her.

"Though life was not always kind to Hester, she always faced the world with a positive outlook, an open mind and a pair of willing hands.

"How difficult it is to find a virtuous woman. Well, we all found one in Hester Allen Street. And we are all richer for it.

"Reverend Toomey will now lead us in prayer."

Thad had only been Hester Street's pastor for a short time, but he expressed gratitude for her "generous spirit." I knew he was referring to her lifestyle of nonjudgmental caring and concern for everyone she knew as well as her generous financial contributions. Every person there knew about the latter. The small church we were sitting in continued to exist because Don and Hester Street continued their contributions there when they moved their membership to the "church in town" so their children could benefit from the activities a bigger church could offer.

The Streets also gave generously to Calvary Church. When Don Street died, gifts in his honor were used to add a prayer chapel with stained glass windows to the church. It was named the Street Memorial Chapel.

As Thad continued to pray, I wondered briefly why I knew who the donors were at the Baptist Churches. From what I remember as a child, Baptists don't have stewardship drives or sign pledge cards— although they do preach a lot on tithing. Yet, everybody in town would tell you that a handful of people, including the Streets and my grandpa, were responsible for the fact that Calvary Baptist has the largest physical plant of any church in town. As far as I know, the donors don't discuss their giving with anybody.

By contrast, while it is true that I'm not the most faithful member of the town's only Methodist Church, it is also true that I don't have the vaguest idea who contributes to the church's budget. We do have a stewardship campaign every fall and plan a budget based on the pledges that come in. That is all I know about the church's finances.

I'm sure Thad would be pleased to know that his prayer moved me to ponder church finances.

My mind returned to Grandpa's eulogy.

I forget sometime that Grandpa had 60 years worth of a life before he was my grandfather. Even though I've seen pictures of him as a young man, it's hard to imagine that the bright eyed 20 year-old in those old sepia-tone pictures is my grandfather. And to think that he had loved a woman before Grandma. Though I never met her, I know from family stories that Grandpa thought his wife could walk on water.

People in this town think my grandfather is the closest thing in Hilltop to a saint. For 70 years, when people are experiencing some of the worst life has to offer, Grandpa has been there to help them through it. In the eyes of most of the town, Ernest Gibbs can do no wrong. When you ask him about this unofficial "sainthood" Grandpa always says, "Saints get a special place in heaven. The only people who have a better spot are the people who had to live with the saints on earth. Surely my Rose has one of the best seats in the house."

My thoughts were interrupted by the Pilgrim's Run Boys' closing hymn.

> Some glad morning when this life is o'er
> I'll fly away
> To a home on God's celestial shore
> I'll fly away
>
>
> Just a few more weary days and then
> I'll fly away
> To a home where joy shall never end
> I'll fly away
>
> I'll fly away oh Glory
> I'll fly away
> When I die Hallelujah by and by
> I'll fly away

At the cemetery, the grave was under a gigantic old umbrella-shaped oak tree that seemed designed to shelter Mrs. Street's body. The service was short, and the Pilgrim's Run Boys sang an *a cappella* rendition of "Beulah Land" that would have convinced any doubter of Mrs. Street's destination.

I'm sure Julia was mortified by the whole thing. And I'm a little ashamed to admit that the thought of her outrage made me smile. I wonder how much of Mrs. Street's planning of her funeral was based on what she wanted and how much of it was based on what she knew would drive her estranged daughter right up the wall.

I had to hand it to Hester Street—she left this world with the same flair she possessed while she was in it.

CHAPTER 14

After the funeral, I had some errands to run before going back to the office. As I drove through the older section of town, I passed the Waltham home and noticed a moving van parked in the driveway. Glenda had told me she was doing some repairs and painting on the inside before moving her things from Florida, so she must have finished at least some of her renovations.

Near the street are two huge pecan trees. I remember going there with my mom to pick up pecans. The Walthams never sold the pecans, but they gave them to anyone who wanted to pick them up. My mom could bake a great pecan pie. We had them a lot before she left because the pecans were so readily available. (In Hilltop we call them pe-KAHNS, not PEE-cans.) It looked like these trees were still producing. I made a note to bake a pie soon. I haven't had one in ages. Maybe I could even score some pecans during my visit.

Beyond the pecans were the stately Magnolia trees that are covered with huge white blossoms in the summer time.

Set in the center of a two or three acre lot, the big white house (which was badly in need of a paint job) has pale yellow shutters. It has a wrap-around porch with a railing that was also in need of some repair. The house was probably built in the 1920s, but it is a copy of some of the antebellum houses in Mississippi and Louisiana. I was sure Glenda would restore it to its original grandeur as soon as she got settled in.

There were still a lot of things I didn't know about this circus-performer-turned-respectable-matron, and I couldn't resist the urge to turn in the driveway.

The door was open with the movers going in and out, so I tapped on the door frame and hollered inside, "Hello, anyone home?"

"Come on in, Lu," Glenda called from somewhere inside the big house. The house has all these little nooks that center around a big spiral staircase leading to the second floor. I made my way around until I found Glenda sitting on the floor sifting through boxes.

"Can I do anything to help?" I asked.

She looked overwhelmed sitting there amid that pile of boxes, propped up against a well-used leather arm chair.

"Thanks," she said. "But the movers are handling the heavy things, and everything else is just stuff I'm going have to figure out what to do with. I would love some company while I sort, though."

I settled myself on the floor.

"I really should have gotten rid of more of Charlie's things before I hauled them all the way from Florida," she said as she pulled from one box what looked to be a brass doorstop in the shape of a fish. She wrinkled her nose.

"Why on earth I packed this, I have no idea. I donated most of the clothes, but I couldn't bear to part with a lot of his things. He's not even been gone a year, and I guess I'm not ready to give all of him up just yet."

"Was your husband a fisherman?" I asked, after she pulled a small print of a fish from the doorstop box.

"Whenever he could get away from work, you'd find him in the bass boat," she said, pausing from her unpacking. "You know he had his heart attack right in the middle of the lake. His buddy got him back to land and called an ambulance. He made it to the hospital, but it was too late. I did get to hold his hand before he went. I'll always be so grateful that his last moments were doing what he loved most and not trying to fix some problem at work or doing some menial chore around the house or something like that."

She paused, "But listen to me. Like you don't get enough of all this kind of talk every day of your life. Here you are blessed with a little time away from your own work, and off I go about people dying!"

"It's okay," I assured her. "I don't like for people to die, but I really do enjoy hearing people talk about the people they've lost. It's kind of nice. Tell me more. What did your husband do?"

"Well, now, that is kind of an interesting story," she said, smiling at the thought. "When I met Charles, he was a construction foreman. He worked for a big company and ran various projects in the area. He made a decent living and really liked what he did. He grew up in Galena where we lived. Like most cities, the downtown area had kind of gone downhill. Shops and businesses moved to the edges of the town where the new mall and shopping areas were. Nobody lived down there, and the only restaurant was this old diner that had been there for years. It was a lot like The Diner here in Hilltop. Good food and good prices, so folks would go out of their way to get there.

"Anyway," she continued. "Charlie came into an unexpected source of funds to buy up part of the area and revamp the place. He put in a bunch of those loft apartments young people like you are so crazy about these days. Renovated old restaurants so these little coffee shops would come in. Someone even opened a sushi bar. Suddenly this little three block area where no one ever went became the place to be.

"The word spread, especially through the people who provided the money to begin with—they have kind of their own network—and people all over Florida, all over the Southeast, really, began to call Charlie to help them revitalize their downtown areas. Instead of a construction foreman, he became a restoration consultant. And let me tell you, consultants make a whole lot more money than foremen!

"Oh, my goodness," she exclaimed. "How absolutely tacky you must think I am, sitting here talking about money like this!"

(In the South, we never talk about how much things cost or how much money people have. It's simply not done.)

"Not at all," I reassured her. "It's obvious you're proud of your husband. You must miss him a lot. Do you have a picture of him? I'd love to see one."

"Oh," she waved her hand over all the boxes. "There's plenty of them around here somewhere."

She took a framed picture from the box.

"Here it is!" she said. "I've been looking for this."

I looked over her shoulder, expecting a photograph of her husband. Instead, I saw a picture of the Waltham house in its "glory days," looking freshly painted and accented by a bank of azaleas in full bloom.

"I knew it was here somewhere," she said. "Wendy sent me this picture while I was still with the circus. I guess he thought he would make me homesick enough to come back. I've kept it with me ever since, and when I married Charlie, I had it framed and hung it in our bedroom. I guess I always knew I would come back here someday."

I tried to be enthusiastic about the picture, but it was not exactly what I was hoping to see. I still wanted to know what her husband was like. I don't know why I cared so much. I guess I was just curious about the man who had so captivated this elegant woman.

She insisted on taking a break and making us a cup of tea, but it was getting late and I still had errands to run. I promised to call her soon for a lunch date.

"I hope you will come back when I get everything moved in and get the outside painted," she said as she walked me to the door. "I'm eager to finish up in the house so I can get started in the yard."

Except for some information about what her husband did for a living, I hadn't learned anything else about Glenda and why she stayed away from Hilltop all these years. Maybe I need to take some lessons from Miss Mattie. And besides all that, I forgot to ask about the pecans.

CHAPTER 15

November finished without major incident. Gibbs Funeral Home had four more funerals during the month, and all of them were older people who had lived good, long lives. In no way do I mean to minimize the grief of the loved ones those four people left behind, but these deaths, while sad, were not a tragedy. In the funeral business, that's what you call a very good month.

A whole week without a single funeral is a rarity in Hilltop where senior citizens seem to make up the majority of residents. I had caught up on all my cards and correspondence and spent a lot of time reading Henri Nouwen's *In Memoriam*. Nouwen is a Catholic priest who was chaplain at Yale University. He wrote the book when his mother died.

When the phone rang, I was sure my "down time" had ended.

It was Harley Thomas. Harley and I have been friends since his wife died two years ago. Nora Thomas was a nurse who worked for a doctor in Stuttgart until she had a stroke that left her partially paralyzed and brain damaged. According to Harley, doctors said the stroke may have been caused by a mixture of prescription drugs. They suspected she was taking the drugs from the samples left at the clinic by pharmaceutical reps. Harley and the people she worked with had no idea that Nora had a drug problem.

After the stroke, the pleasant, fun-loving woman Harley had loved for most of his life changed personalities. She was constantly agitated and difficult, and sometimes violent. Harley hired women to stay with her during the day while he worked as a building contractor. He spent all his non-working hours with her, taking her to the beauty shop on Saturdays, and, when she would go, wheeling her to the Methodist Church on Sunday. A lot of women wondered out loud why he didn't put her in a nursing home so he could "get on with his life."

Harley's response was: "When we married, we made some vows that included 'in sickness and in health' and 'till death do us part.' And neither of us has died yet."

When Nora had the stroke that took her life, I was amazed at the grief and tenderness Harley expressed as he made the arrangements. He sent his sister out to buy a new pink dress.

"She always looked pretty in pink," he said.

And when he looked at her in the casket, he whispered, "What I wouldn't give to hear her curse me just one more time."

Later he told me, "Even before the stroke, she was a feisty one. That's one of the things I loved about her."

The widows in the community saw the way Harley treated Nora during her illness, and they know a good catch when they see one. The dinner invitations and the drop-in casseroles in dishes-that-had-to-be-returned came quickly and steadily for a year after Nora's death. Harley was kind (and put on about 15 pounds), but he never expressed any interest in any of the ladies that came by. He missed the Nora he had married. He participated in one of our grief support groups shortly after she died, and he continued to stop by the office periodically to talk to me about her.

"I need to talk to you about something personal," he said today. "Is this a good time?"

I told him I had a lunch appointment in about half an hour, so we settled on a one-thirty meeting in the office. He assured me that it wasn't business. It's always nice to have someone come to talk about a subject other than funerals and dying, and I was curious.

I was having lunch with the Reverend Karen Raymond to discuss our plans for the holiday grief seminar scheduled to begin the first week in December. In addition to being pastor of the Episcopal Church, Karen is my best friend and soul mate in Hilltop. We didn't meet until I moved back here to work at the funeral home. She was one of the first people to congratulate me on my new job.

I have to admit, even I was a little taken aback when this pretty, petite young woman walked into my office in a skirt and clerical collar.

The first thing she said to me was, "So glad to have another woman here in Hilltop who holds a job where people expect to see a man."

She had arrived in Hilltop about six months before I came back, and she had the privilege of being the first woman most of the residents of our fair town had ever seen behind a pulpit. It's not just that she's a woman—she's an attractive woman. Folks around here probably could have taken to a nice, matronly-looking female priest just fine, but they were pretty sure that a preacher wasn't supposed to be as cute as Karen is.

At about 5 foot 2, Karen stands on a wooden milk crate when she preaches so that her face, framed by a dark, short, stylish 'do,' can be seen over the pulpit. Folks like the fact that she's married, but they did have to get used to the fact that Karen's last name is Raymond and her husband is Bill Carpenter. There was some discussion about just how committed a woman could be to a man whose name she is not willing to take. I think there is at least one elderly member of the congregation who still believes they are living in sin because she doesn't understand how you can be married and have different names.

There were skeptics (even among the liberal Episcopalians), but Karen won everyone over. Her cheerfulness is nothing short of infectious. Besides her demeanor, Karen possesses qualities that don't match her age. I don't know how to describe it except to say that she's just wise.

We met at The Diner ostensibly to go over the upcoming grief seminar sessions, but really just to catch up. Karen was wearing a pair of bright red leggings and a Christmas sweater with the words "I Believe" on it. I would have looked like a giant elf wanna-be in that outfit, but she looked adorable. We had just sat down to eat when Joan McNair came in with her sister Janice Street. They waved as they came in and sat at a booth on the other side of the restaurant.

"I didn't know Janice was back in town," I said to Karen.

"She's actually here to stay," Karen said.

Joan's family goes to the Episcopal Church, and Karen and Margaret are good friends.

"Mrs. Street left a hefty estate. She divided it equally among the three girls, with a good amount left in trust for the grandchildren—I think Margaret and her two cousins can access the money when they turn 35. Even though she divided the money equally, Mrs. Street left the house and all of its contents to Janice. Joan told me she knew all about it before her mother died. I don't know how that sister from back east feels about it, but apparently she's not putting up a fuss.

"Anyway," Karen continued. "Janice is going to quit both her jobs at the end of the school term and move to Hilltop permanently. She must have taken a leave or something to come home and get the estate settled."

I watched the two sisters as they ordered. They talked and laughed as they waited. I wondered why Janice never married. She's an attractive lady and seems to be very personable. Margaret really likes her. Even when we were in school together, she reveled in the trips to St. Louis to visit her Aunt Janice. I'm as liberated as the next person, but let's face it—we live in a world of couples. When someone manages to avoid becoming a couple by the time she is 55 years old, people wonder why. Being single apparently isn't a problem for Janice. She's seen more of the world than most people even know exists, and she's had a long and successful career doing what she loves. I wondered if I would be that gracious if I am still single at 55.

Karen and I caught up on a little more gossip and munched on the veggie platter of the day—fried okra, butter beans, fresh sliced tomatoes and corn on the cob. We shared a basket of cornbread. They have great cornbread at The Diner. No sugar. Over at The Club Car they put sugar in their cornbread so it tastes like a muffin or a corn cake—not something you want to mix with butter beans or peas. Sugar in cornbread—it's just wrong.

Karen and I made plans for her and Bill and Jim Pat and me to get together for dinner on Friday night. We usually do something like that about every other weekend, but it had been a month since we had all gotten together. With Advent season coming up for Karen and the cold and flu season beginning for Jim Pat, we figured we better get in some recreation time while we could.

As we left the restaurant, I stopped by to speak to Joan and Janice.

"I hear you're going to be a Hilltop resident," I said to Janice. "We're glad to have you."

She laughed. "Guess there aren't many secrets in Hilltop. I'll have to get used to that again. The school knows I won't be coming back next semester. I think 30 years is long enough for anyone to teach school. I'm really going to miss my church and the choir though."

"We sure could use another organist in town to play at funerals— and weddings," I added. "I do hope you're not retiring completely?"

"Not at all," she smiled. "Put me on the list!"

CHAPTER 16

After lunch I went back to the office to meet with Harley. He arrived on time in pressed, dark jeans and one of his many plaid shirts tucked in over a stomach that had seen one too many potluck dinners. But who am I to talk? At 60, with his salt-and-pepper hair and muscular build, Harley is a nice looking man. As soon as he walked in my office, he got right to the point.

"Joan and Bill McNair invited me to dinner last night, and her sister Janice was there. You know we went to grammar school together more years ago than I'd care to admit. Lu, this is the first woman I've met since Nora died that I'd like to see socially."

He stopped, waiting for a response, so I said, "I really like Janice. In fact, I just ran into her at lunch. She's a lovely woman. Why don't you just ask her out?"

I wondered if the fact that she has never married bothered him.

"I would," he said, "but everybody in Hilltop knows she inherited a fortune, and I don't want her to think I'm after her money."

Experience has taught me not to laugh even when a situation strikes me as funny. I couldn't imagine anyone viewing Harley as a gold digger. How much money does a man need to buy flannel shirts and drive a pick-up? Of all the problems I could have anticipated, this was at the bottom of the list. I waited a moment, but he didn't say anything else. He obviously expected a response.

"Harley," I said, "aren't you getting a little ahead of yourself? This is the nineties. A date does not a life-long commitment make. Why don't you just ask her out to dinner? You could even take Joan and Bill along if that would make it easier."

He was silent for a few seconds, then he laughed—a deep, booming laugh that made his face flush.

"Dadgummit, you're right, Lu," he admitted. "Can't be any harm in taking a lady to dinner, now can there? I guess I've just been out of the dating game too long. You know, Nora and I married at 18. Come to think of it, I don't guess I was ever in the dating game!"

He stood up and took my hand. "Thanks, Lu."

He started to walk out the door, but paused and turned around.

"You know, after Nora died, you were such a blessing to me," he began. "I was so grief-stricken I forgot to tell you what a great man your Pa is."

I looked at him questioningly. I know that I think my dad is great, but I didn't know that other people shared that opinion. Dad's such a quiet guy. Not many people really know him, and I didn't know that he and Harley had ever been close.

"Not long before Nora had her stroke, I took out a loan to put up a building of my own. I was going to put in one of those super station gas places right across from the washateria. You know, the kind that also sells sandwiches and ice cream and little plastic toys and such. I had used part of the money to buy into a franchise and have an architect draw up the plans when the rain set in. You remember that April? It rained almost two weeks straight. Not only did it delay the work, but the bulldozer I rented to clear the land literally got stuck in the mud. Couldn't get it out for almost a week after the rain stopped. Then the thing with Nora happened. I just scrapped the plans; but with her medical bills and all, I had no idea how I was going to pay that money back. I was getting further and further behind on my payments. I'm a man who pays his debts. I've never run out on any of my obligations. I was so worried that I couldn't sleep at night. Everyone thought I looked so awful because of Nora. But I had given her problem over to the Lord. Somehow it didn't seem right to burden the Lord with my money problems too."

I still couldn't imagine what this had to do with my dad. But it's standard operating procedure when telling a story here in Hilltop to go around the world to get to the actual point. I knew Harley would get there eventually.

"One night, pretty late, I just called your dad at home and said, 'Bobby, I'm just worried sick about not being able to make the payments on my loan.' I told him about the medical bills and the delays caused by the rain.

"'I'm so worried I can't sleep at night,' I told him, 'and it's making me sick. I don't know what to do.'

"And do you know what your dad said?

"'Well, Harley,' he said. 'I'm up now, and I'll worry about this 'til at least sunup. No sense in both of us sittin' up and worrying, so why don't you just go on to bed and get a good night's sleep. I'll take it from here.'

"Lu, it was the first good night's sleep I'd had in a long time. Your dad, as Nora would say, is a full-yard wide and all wool."

And with that he walked out of my office before I could think how to respond. After about a minute I picked up the phone and dialed.

"Dad, it's me. What are you doing tonight? Why don't you come over for dinner?"

Anne Russ and Nancy Russ

CHAPTER 17

The holidays were rapidly approaching, and I spent part of the day at home catching up on a few chores—today was technically my day off. My humble abode is not exactly grand in size, so when any part of it gets messy or dirty, the whole place looks bad. By the time I finished a couple of loads of laundry, gave the bathroom a good scrubbing and vacuumed the carpets, it was time to head out to my tutoring session.

I put my hair up and jumped in the shower to wash off the lovely mixture of dust and Pine Sol that had stuck to my body. In my bathroom oasis, it's really hard to be quick about anything, but I knew I'd be late if I lingered too long. I by-passed the pantsuits and put on a pair of jeans and my favorite old sweater. It's starting to unravel at the bottom, but it's far too soft and comfy to discard.

Generally, I walk from my place to the Boys and Girls Club, but the sky looked like it was tuning up to storm, so I jumped in the Honda and was there in about three minutes.

The Boys and Girls Club of Greater Hilltop coordinates tutoring sessions after school for any young person who wishes to take advantage of them. As burned out as I was when I left St. Louis, I didn't want to completely give up my contact with young people. I'm kind of a standing chaperone at the high school for field trips. Because I have some control over my schedule, I usually head somewhere with a group of rowdy teenagers about three times each semester. I also tutor once a week at the Club.

I don't claim to be any great scholar, but as long as I stay at about the junior high level, I can pretty much hold my own with whatever the kids bring to me. This semester I had Casey, a 13-year-old eighth grader who is a dead ringer for what I've always imagined Huckleberry Finn to look like—brown hair in constant need of a haircut, freckles sprinkled across his nose and big blue eyes full of devilment. Even when he puts on his best "I'm being serious" face, his eyes give him away—some sort of mischief is brewing in his head.

Casey has no sense of history. At least, as a subject, he has trouble making sense of it. All those events, dates and people just seem to get jumbled up in his head. He's got all the information, but somehow the wires get crossed up there. It doesn't help that at the junior high, the history teachers also teach geography. At the beginning of the year, the teacher had them studying the discovery of America and memorizing the state capitals at the same time. So on the test, when Casey was asked where Christopher Columbus landed, he put down Ohio. Like I said, the wires get crossed.

Today's topic was presidents—well, actually one president. Everyone in Casey's class had to do a report on a president. Because everyone wanted one of the "well-knowns," the teacher made the kids take the luck of the draw. And apparently, Casey was fresh out of luck. He drew Chester A. Arthur—a man who was never even elected to the office. In fact, he wasn't even qualified to run for president because he was born in Canada. The only way he made his way into the highest office of our land was that he occupied the second highest office when President Garfield was shot by a religious fanatic who had been denied a government job. (Lest you think me a history whiz, I must confess, I never heard of Chester A. Arthur before Casey brought his name to my attention. The above info can be found in any standard encyclopedia.)

Casey was not particularly concerned that he had drawn an "unknown." He figured he knew about as much about Arthur as he knew about any of the rest of them except maybe Washington and Lincoln.

"Lu, isn't Arthur the one that put a round table in the oval office," he asked.

For a minute, knowing how he often gets his wires crossed, I thought he was serious. But I looked at his eyes and realized that Casey was trying to hook me.

Frankly, I thought Casey was up against a toughie. The focus of the project had to be on the major contribution of the president to which you were assigned. This guy had never even been elected! So I had stopped by our local library to see what I could dig up on Chet. Casey is supposed to do his own research, but I figured I needed to be in the know if I was going to be of any help.

For a town our size, Hilltop is blessed with one of the best little libraries in the country. Jim Pat had a maiden great-aunt who had inherited the Whitney family home. Their family was hurt just as bad as everyone else when the market crashed, but apparently Aunt Rhetta hadn't put all her eggs in one basket. When she died, her will directed her attorney and family to a safe hidden in the back of a closet. Along with the combination to the safe were instructions to use the large sum of cash in it to convert her home into a town library. I don't know the exact sum, but it was enough to renovate the house, stock it with books and still have money left over for an endowment that adds new books each year and pays the salary of a full time librarian. It's a wonderful place and I go there whenever I get the chance.

However, I feared that even our well-stocked library wasn't going to help me help Casey with Chester A. Arthur. But bless his little heart, the man made good use of his time in office. He was the first president to introduce legislation that made our Civil Service program what it is today. He was the first guy to insist that federal jobs be given out on merit rather than based on who you know. He pushed legislation that created the Civil Service Commission which required competitive exams to determine who got highly desirable government jobs. If that doesn't have the makings of a great report, I don't know what does. Convincing Casey that working for the postal service or the IRS or the Department of Motor Vehicles is a desirable vocation was the hardest part of getting started.

Casey finally conceded that a steady paycheck with good benefits is a desirable, if somewhat unromantic aspiration, and he settled in to compose his masterpiece on President Arthur. Confident that Casey was well on his way to an A+ report, I headed home—by way of the pharmacy.

The storm that was threatening earlier in the afternoon was making good on that threat in a big way. The rain came down in sheets, and a strong wind threatened to topple the tall pine trees near the streets. The jagged streaks of lightning that lit up the sky would have been beautiful had they not been accompanied by ominous claps of thunder that seemed to shake the earth beneath my little Honda. I'm not reckless when it comes to bad weather, but we have storms like this spring up often enough that I don't think that much about it. I just drove a little slower and turned the windshield wipers up to top speed.

I ran in the pharmacy just ahead of a big boom of thunder that was so close it rattled the shop's windows.

"Gosh, Lu," Jim Pat said. "What the heck are you doing out in all this?"

"It's tutoring day," I told him. "I was already out before it got 'like this'. I just came by to see if we could get together with Karen and Bill on Friday."

"Sure," he said. "We haven't gone out with them in a while. Sounds good."

"Are you leaving here at 6?" I asked.

He nodded.

"Why don't you come over to my house, and we'll cook up some chili and hide out from the storm."

"Couldn't think of a better way to ride out a storm," he said, grinning at me.

Lord have mercy, my stomach still does flip flops when that man grins at me. I hope it always does.

"Be careful," he yelled as I headed back out into the storm.

When I got home, I started on the chili right away. One good thing about people who love to eat—most of us love to cook. I was going to make my extra-special chili. As the ground turkey was browning (no need to clog arteries unnecessarily), I started chopping up fresh tomatoes and bell peppers. Then I broke out my secret stash of Vidalia onions. I always buy a ton of them when they're in season, and they keep a long time if you keep them in a cool dry place. I also chop some and put then in the freezer for year-round use. Vidalias are the only onions I can chop without my eyes stinging so badly that I have to leave the room. To all these ingredients, I added two cans of black beans—they give chili a completely different flavor from the maroon-colored legumes typically used in such a concoction. After tossing in a good dose of my secret spices and some not-for-wimps *habanera* hot sauce, I set the pot on simmer, popped my favorite Christine Kane CD into the stereo, and curled up on the couch with the latest Patricia Cornwell book to wait for Jim Pat. I was on call, but I was hoping that even the Grim Reaper would have sense enough to stay in on a night like tonight.

CHAPTER 18

Jim Pat arrived just as I was pulling the "home made" Pop-N-Fresh bread out of the oven. He made all the obligatory 'smells good' and 'looks great' comments, and we sat down to eat. I think I may have overdone the pepper, because it wasn't long before we were both using our napkins to wipe our runny noses. Just before our eyes started to tear, my beeper went off.

Jim Pat and I exchanged the same looks we always do when my beeper goes off. My look says, "I'm sorry this is ruining our date" and his look says, "It's your job. What can you do?"

I recognized the number as our local hospital. Hilltop is very proud of Memorial Hospital. We've worked hard to keep it here. It's really a very small clinic staffed by EMTs, a couple of midwives, a nurse practitioner and a physician's assistant. Doc Green is the official attending physician, and the hospital we're affiliated with in Memphis sends a different specialist over here each day of the week. You can always tell which doctor is here by the people in the waiting room. The teenagers take the place over on Mondays when the dermatologist is here. On Wednesday, the arthritis specialist comes and the older folks line up. A local garden club actually had to change their Wednesday meeting to Thursday—that's pediatrician day, which doesn't pose any conflict to the retired population of the green thumb group.

I called in and got Doc Green himself. "Sorry to bother you, Lu," he apologized. "But this is a bad one. It's Terry Phillips."

Doc Green was right—it was bad. Terry Phillips is Hilltop's golden child. He's the star player on the basketball team, straight "A" student and all-around poster boy for the kind of kids Hilltop could produce.

"What happened?" I asked. "Was it a car wreck?"

"No," he said. "Something far more bizarre. Apparently Terry had been mowing the lawn earlier today and had taken a break to finish some homework. When it started storming, he went outside to pull the lawn mower in, and he was hit by lightening. I believe he died instantly."

"You're kidding," I said, realizing what an insensitive comment it was the instant I said it. Of course, the doctor wasn't kidding.

"I only wish I were," he replied. "Mo is coming to the hospital to pick up the body. There's nothing you can do tonight, but I thought you might want some time to prepare yourself for the boy's family coming in to plan the funeral."

As soon as I got off the phone with Doc Green, I called over to the Phillips house. Karen is their priest, and I figured she'd be there. Sure enough, she picked up the phone.

"I was just going to call you," she said. "How did you find out?"

After I explained that Doc Green had called from the hospital, I asked what I could do to help.

"Just try to prepare yourself for tomorrow," Karen said. "I don't know what to tell you other than to pray. I thought I was something of an expert at helping people through grief and tragedy. Lord knows I've seen enough of it. But this beats anything I've ever seen. I actually don't even know if the Phillips will come to plan the funeral tomorrow. They're in shock. Mrs. Phillips wouldn't even look at the body at the hospital. She was sobbing so hard she began to hyperventilate. Doc Green gave her a sedative, but even that took about an hour to kick in. About half-an-hour ago Mr. Phillips announced that he'd be damned if he was going to plan the funeral of his own son, and then he locked himself in the bedroom and refuses to leave. I'm going to stay here tonight with Trish. You know Terry's little sister, right?"

"Yes," I said. "We've hung out at the Club before. How is she?"

Considering what's happened to her brother, and the state her parents are in, she's doing as well as anyone could expect. We've been sitting here talking about Terry and crying," Karen went on. "I think Trish may be the only one who emerges from this tragedy intact."

"Well, let me know if I can do anything beyond praying."

Soon after I hung up with Doc Green, Grandpa showed up at the door.

"Sorry to bother you and Jim Pat," he apologized. "But I guess you heard."

I nodded.

"This is the toughest one to come along since you've been here," he said. "Would you like me to handle it?"

"No," I said. "I would like you to be there. You always know what to say, but I think I need to learn how to do this."

"Well, I've already decided one thing," he said. "We're doing this funeral at no charge. The last thing the Phillips need right now is to have to scrape up the money to bury their son. We'll write off all our expenses and do it right."

The Phillips both worked at the school. Mr. Phillips had been the janitor ever since I was in school and Mrs. Phillips ran the school cafeteria. They made a living, but that was all.

Jim Pat and I finished our chili, but we didn't taste it. When we finished, we just left the dishes on the table and cuddled up on the couch together. I guess I fell asleep. The next thing I knew the sun was shining through the windows, and I was lying on the couch covered with a blanket. The dishes were put away, and I found the leftover chili covered in the fridge.

"What a guy," I thought as I stretched and got to my feet. This was not the first time our date had been cut short by a phone call, and we both knew it probably wouldn't be the last. I squared my shoulders and headed to the shower to get ready for what I knew would be one tough day.

Soon after I got to the office, Karen showed up with Terry's younger sister, Trish. Trish looked like her brother with longer hair. Right now it was just hanging limply on her shoulders. She was wearing a T-shirt that swallowed her, and I guessed it belonged to her big brother. The elder Phillips were not with them. Trish was my first tutoring student at the Boys and Girls Club when I first moved back into town. She's a sweet kid, but she's done just about everything she's big enough to do and then some.

"Lu, can I talk to you for a minute?" Karen asked. She looked like she hadn't slept in a week. She had big bags under her eyes and her whole body just kind of sagged. I'd never seen her look so the opposite of perky.

"Sure," I said. I gave Trish a hug. "Why don't you go have a seat in my office? We'll be there in a minute."

"The parents aren't coming," Karen whispered. "I've never had this happen, nor have I ever heard of it happening, but the Phillips refuse to have anything to do with planning their son's funeral. They're in some sort of denial squared to the Nth degree!"

I just stood there staring at her for awhile.

"Why is Trish here?" I finally asked.

"She's here to make the arrangements," Karen answered. "Can you believe it? She actually volunteered. I tried to talk to the parents, to make them understand that this was far too much to put on a child that doesn't even yet possess a driver's license, but they wouldn't listen. And she insisted."

"Okay," I said, sort of to myself, letting it sink in that I had to plan a funeral with a child whose brother had just died. "Trish and I have always had a good rapport; let's see what we can come up with."

Karen and I went back to my office. Trish, almost swallowed by my overstuffed couch, was staring at the floor clutching a folded-up piece of notebook paper.

"I'm so sorry about what happened to your brother," I said softly, sitting down next to her. "I know you'll miss him very much. Are you sure you want to do this now? We can't put it off forever, but we don't have to do this today. Maybe your parents will change their minds and want to be involved in a few days."

"No," she said. "They won't. I don't even know if they'll come to the funeral. They can't bear the thought of my brother being gone. I can't either. But I owe it to my parents to do something, and I owe it to my brother. We promised each other the perfect funeral."

Perfect funeral?

"You remember back last year when those boys down in El Dorado were killed trying to beat the train across the tracks?" she asked.

Karen and I both nodded.

"Well, Terry had gone to basketball camp with two of them every summer since they were all eight years old. Some of the guys on the team here even went down to the funeral. Terry said it was awful. There were flowers all over the caskets. The preacher was using words nobody understood, and the music! Terry said if those boys weren't already dead, they would've died if they had known what their funerals were like."

She paused and looked sheepishly at me.

"Sorry," she said. "Bad joke."

"No worries," I said, using the typical phrase the kids bat around at the club these days. "As long as you can make a joke and laugh a little, you know you're going to be okay."

"Well, Terry figured Karen would do a much better job of the funeral than the minister at those guys' funeral," she said. "And he wanted the coach to make the speech. I can't remember what you call it."

"The eulogy," Karen offered.

"Yeah," Trish nodded. "That's it. He doesn't want any flowers. He said with all the money people spent on flowers the basketball gym could have gotten a new floor. And then he wanted to play this song by Green Day. Is it okay to play non-church music in the church? I have the words right here."

She unfolded a typewritten piece of paper and handed it to Karen and me.

> *Good Riddance (Time of Your Life)*
> Another turning point, a fork stuck in the road.
> Time grabs you by the wrist, directs you where to go.
> So make the best of this test, and don't ask why.
> It's not a question, but a lesson learned in time.
> It's something unpredictable, but in the end is right.
> I hope you had the time of your life.
> So take the photographs, and still frames in your mind.
> Hang it on a shelf of good health and good time.
> Tattoos of memories and dead skin on trial.
> For what it's worth, it was worth all the while.
> It's something unpredictable, but in the end is right
> I hope you had the time of your life.
> I hope you had the time of your life.

"I think that'll be just fine," Karen smiled. "I believe God would approve."

Anne Russ and Nancy Russ

CHAPTER 19

The funeral was the next day. It was a dreary, gray, mid-December day. I kept thinking about that old hymn, "In the Bleak Mid-Winter". We were certainly there. I hate it when the weather is bad for funerals. Death is depressing enough without the weather adding to it. Although, I have to admit that it would have seemed inappropriate—almost obscene—for the sun to be shining on such a wretched day.

The Episcopal Church was packed with people—about half of them teenagers. I knew that this was a first funeral for many of them. What a horrible way to have to greet death for the first time. The first time you go to a funeral it should be one for your 95-year-old aunt who had an absolutely fabulous life and died peacefully in her sleep.

I knew Coach Cox was nervous about "giving the speech" as Trish put it. If he could handle the actual speaking part, I knew he'd do okay. The coach is a fairly religious man who sings in the choir at the Calvary Baptist Church. Since Jim Pat's dad is his boss, I've had a chance to spend a little time with him at athletic department gatherings. He's quite the amateur chef. He makes these fabulous little appetizers with water chestnuts wrapped in bacon. He's just okay at coaching basketball, but he's fantastic at coaching kids. He really loves all the guys and girls that play for him. I couldn't imagine how he was going to get through this eulogy.

After the Green Day song played, the coach got up. He stood at the pulpit for what seemed like forever before he started to speak.

"Ever since Trish asked me to speak here today, I've been trying to come up with the answer to the question that me and everybody else is asking. Why? I've wrestled and thought and prayed, almost without ceasing, but I couldn't come up with an answer. I can't imagine and I don't understand why this had to happen. Sometimes I think that's what Heaven will be—a place where we find out the answers to all the things we didn't understand on earth. And then other times I think that the beauty of heaven will be that we won't need to understand anymore. Everything we thought was important while we were here just won't seem so crucial anymore.

79

"One thing I do know about heaven—Terry Phillips is up there right now. I know that just as sure as I know that the sun is going to come up tomorrow morning. And if you believe heaven is whatever you want it to be, then I guess for Terry, heaven is one endless pick-up basketball game with occasional breaks for pizza.

"We can mourn the fact that Terry will never grow into full manhood. But know that we are mourning for us—mourning the fact that such a fine person is now missing from our midst. Terry is now in a place so grand and wonderful that if we could fully understand, we might even be jealous. But we don't understand. We're human. And we miss our friend, our brother and our son.

"One thing we can rejoice in today is Terry's life. Though it was short, he used his time well. And if we want to do right by Terry, we'll go on using our time well. Not to do so would make this tragedy even more tragic. Living every day to the fullest and remembering how precious life is will keep Terry Phillips alive in our hearts forever. God bless you all."

The coach couldn't miss my tear-stained, mouth-agape face as he walked back to his seat. I'd never heard the man string more than two sentences together. Seeing my surprise, he leaned over and whispered, "It wasn't me, Lu. I asked the Lord to give me the words and the voice, and I reckon he did just that."

I just stood there, still stunned from the death of our town hero and marveling at the unlikely places from which the Grace of God makes itself known.

As I walked down the aisle of the church, I saw Terry's parents sitting near the back. Mrs. Phillips was sobbing quietly, and Mr. P. stood with his arm around her shoulder. His face was so white I thought he might just crumble any second. At Karen's brief graveside service it was Trish who comforted her parents and greeted people, thanking them for coming.

CHAPTER 20

The next morning dawned bright and sunny in spite of lower-than-average temperatures for December. I woke up thinking of the Phillips, especially Trish. It was going to be hard for all of them to return to the school where Terry had been in the center of everything.

I went to the office early, thinking I would spend some time getting myself together before I tackled the plans for the upcoming grief seminar. I had only been there for a few minutes when someone tapped lightly on the door and a head full of corkscrew curls poked its way around the door frame.

If there was ever a person who can brighten a day, it's Emily Peartree. I was surprised to see her since there were no funerals planned. I see her when we have work for her or when I go for my monthly standing appointment to get my mane trimmed.

"You got a minute?" she asked. My first reaction was to hope she wasn't resigning. Emily can talk non-stop when she and Mo are working together, but she's actually kind of shy around the rest of us. She's always there when we need her, always smiling in that bubbly way of hers, but never intrusive. She was just the antidote I needed today.

"Sure," I told her. "Come on in and sit down."

The big chair opposite my desk almost swallowed her. She got straight to the point.

"I need a suggestion. January will be the fifth anniversary of Mama's death, and we—all the Tree kids—want to do something special for a memorial."

Could it really have been five years ago? I couldn't believe it, and told Emily as much.

"I know," she said. "Me neither. I still talk to her so much, sometimes I forget that she's not really here."

Helen Peartree was a Hilltop icon. When she graduated, she went off to college for one semester then came home and married her high school sweetheart. Joe was a cattle farmer, and he and his family owned a big chunk of the rich bottomlands surrounding Hilltop. Helen loved babies, and Joe loved kids; so over the next 15 to 20 years, they had ten children. When the youngest was four months old and the oldest was in high school, Buddy had a "routine" operation on his knee, got a staph infection, and died. The young widow was left with a sprawling ranch house full of children and her grief.

But the grief had to be set aside. The children came first. Both sets of grandparents did what they could to help, but it was not Helen's style to be dependent or conforming. I never knew how she supported all her brood. They weren't wealthy, but they always seemed to have as much as anyone else in the community.

I remember thinking how wonderful it would be to have her for a mom. The atmosphere at her house was very relaxed—totally chaotic, but not frenzied or stressful.

It also wasn't quiet. Crying babies never ruffled Mrs. Peartree.

"Develops their lungs," she would say.

The laundry never got "put up." Each of the many bedrooms had two clothes baskets. Dirty clothes went in one; clean ones in the other. Everyone found something to wear. If they wanted it pressed, they did it themselves.

In spite of the fact that there were so many of them, the Peartree kids didn't fight much. The older ones helped with the younger ones as soon as they got up big enough to run around. They were a close-knit group and were very protective of their mother and each other.

Mama Tree (as everyone in the community called her) was a good cook, and her pots of one-dish meals always held enough to include anyone who happened to be there at mealtime.

When the last of her children started to school, Helen got a part time job as receptionist at the local welfare office. She quickly learned that there was a shortage of foster parents, especially for infants—and she figured she was more qualified than most for the job. She provided temporary homes for a number of infants before they were placed for adoption.

Emily was the first non-infant she got. She was three years old and was in foster care because her mother tended to abuse Emily when she was drunk, which was most of the time. Mama Tree's place was to be temporary while the mother went through a treatment program. But, soon after entering treatment, the mother was diagnosed with liver disease and died.

When Emily was five, a man showed up at Helen's door, claiming to be Emily's father. He had come "to take his daughter home."

Helen didn't like his looks, and she told him he would have to get a court order to get Emily. When the man didn't come back, Helen got her own lawyer and sued for custody of Emily. She not only got custody but was able to legally adopt her when nobody contested her request.

In addition to her two boys, who were in high school, Helen had a little girl again. And this time she had plenty of time for her.

Emily was a "girly" girl. She loved wearing dresses and bows in her hair. Helen's girls had grown up with their brothers, climbing trees and playing the sports their dad had loved. They rode horses and entered rodeos; in the summertime they played softball.

During the school year, they played basketball. Boy, could they play basketball! That was one area where Hilltop was ahead of the rest of the country. Long before the WNBA was even on the drawing board, the Hilltop Lady Hornets were all the rage and the Tree girls were always the star players. I remember going with my parents to watch the girls' games. We even went to Little Rock one year to watch our team win the state championships, and two of the starting players were Peartree girls. Had they come along a decade or so later, any one of them could have given Lisa Leslie a run for her money.

But Emily was a dainty little thing, and Mama Tree got to show off her talents as a dressmaker. Instead of playing sports, Emily entered beauty pageants and played piano. Her mama and her older brothers and sisters were always there to encourage her. Everybody saw Emily as "one lucky little girl."

Then the February of Emily's senior year in high school, the unthinkable happened. I still can't believe it. Mama Tree was coming home from visiting a friend in the hospital in Shreveport. We don't get much snow here at all, but that winter we had more than our usual share of ice and snow. A car meeting Helen Tree's little Toyota wagon hit an icy patch, went out of control and skidded head-on into the Toyota. Mama Tree was killed instantly.

Emily was devastated, but she had a whole passel of people who considered her family and made sure she was taken care of. In fact, the whole town kind of looked upon Emily as "ours" and would do anything for her. I was certainly going to try to do what I could to help with whatever kind of memorial she wanted for Mama Tree.

"With this being the fifth anniversary and all," Emily went on. "We wanted to do something special to remember Mama."

"That's a wonderful idea," I said. "I'm sure everybody will appreciate it. Everyone loved your mom so much."

The whole town had been grief stricken after the accident. It just about did even Grandpa in. I was about to begin my second semester of grad school, and Grandpa called and asked me to come home. He managed to get through the actual funeral, but right after the burial, he went to bed for a week. I stayed and managed the business end of Gibbs while he was recovering. It was my first taste of the family business, and even though I didn't come back until more than three years later, the seed was planted.

"What can I do to help?" I asked Emily.

"I was hoping you could give us a suggestion about what exactly to do," she said. "The other girls and I have been talking about it, and we thought you might have some ideas. We want to do something special, but we don't want it to be morbid or tacky."

"Tacky" is about the worst thing you can be in the South. Tacky is not limited to race, sex, education level or socio-economic status. Anyone can be tacky. Tacky is wearing white shoes after Labor Day or serving chicken salad with dark meat or wearing too much jewelry, or marrying less than a year after the death of a spouse. It reflects badly on you as well as on your family, who obviously didn't teach you any better.

"We thought about making a donation to a charity in her name," Emily continued. "But we don't have enough money to fund a building or any kind of lasting program, and we kind of want something permanent that will have her name on it, so our kids and their kids and grandkids will see it."

I thought for a moment. The answer seemed obvious.

"Now don't think I'm being tongue-in-cheek or disrespectful here," I warned Emily. "But what about a tree? You could plant one of those Bradford pear trees or a Red Maple like the one on our lawn here."

I read somewhere that in some cultures, it is a custom to plant trees as memorials when people die.

Emily's little body bounced out of the chair.

"That's a great idea!" she said. Maybe we could plant it on the courthouse lawn where lightning killed that tree last spring. I'll call the others right away. Thanks, Lu. You're a doll. I knew you'd think of something."

By the time she said "something," she was out the door.

Every problem should be so easy.

Anne Russ and Nancy Russ

CHAPTER 21

The first Monday evening in December we started our annual grief support group. It will meet once a week until the end of January. We meet at the Episcopal Church, but everybody is invited. We send announcements to every family that has experienced a death in the past year and to anyone who has attended the meetings in the past. This year the local newspaper ran a feature article and interviewed the Rev. Karen Raymond on dealing with grief during the holidays.

Grandpa always attends the sessions. His presence seems to have a comforting effect on people—especially people in crisis. But Karen is the leader. I don't go to all the sessions, but since it is an open group, I attend at least a couple of the eight meetings.

We always serve food—sometimes it is just coffee, soft drinks and finger foods. The fact that by the end of the sessions the group is planning potluck dinners supports my theory about the connection between food and (well, maybe not death) but certainly comfort. At the final session, Gibbs provides a full meal, catered by the town's best caterer. (Okay, there are only two caterers in town, but we always use the best.)

At this first session, Grandpa welcomed about 30 people, all of whom were wearing name tags. Grandpa and I knew all of them, but not all of them knew each other. Prior experience has taught us that most of them will bond for life before the sessions end.

Several people, including Harley, had attended the sessions before. Contrary to what some people believe, there are no specific parameters for the grieving period. Unfortunately (or fortunately?), human emotions don't always cooperate with the arbitrary times set for "getting on with life."

I was a little surprised but very glad to see Mr. and Mrs. Phillips there. Mrs. Phillips looked about 10 years older than she used to. Mr. Phillips is a tall man, but his whole body just kind of slumped, making him look shorter. He certainly looked defeated. My own emotions about Terry were still raw, and I couldn't even imagine what his parents must be feeling. Molly Moorehead sat next to Mrs. Phillips.

87

After Grandpa introduced Karen, he joined me at the back of the room. Karen was dressed simply in khaki pants and a periwinkle sweater set. She began by having the participants move their chairs into some semblance of a circle. She feels it is important that people sit close enough to touch each other if they want to. Molly moved her chair closer to Harriet Phillips'.

"I'm going to share briefly a few things I've learned about grief," Karen began, "and then I am going to give you an opportunity to share your experience. I hope every person here will feel free to say anything you want to share, but I also want to emphasize that it's okay not to talk it you don't want to.

"One thing I have observed in my ministry and had confirmed by grief counselors that I have read or worked with is that people who talk about their grief do better than those who don't. We live in a culture that encourages all of us (especially men) to 'keep a stiff upper lip,' 'don't cry out loud,' as the song says. But I can tell you grief will not stay contained. People who grieve privately and silently often find themselves wondering where that depression, or migraine headaches, or even a rash is coming from. It's just possible that these are the outward signs of grief working itself out. Talking about grief with people you trust can definitely speed the healing process.

"A second observation I would make is that every person is unique, and your grief is unique. Don't compare the depth of your grief or the place you are in your grieving with where someone else is. Your relationship with the person you lost is unique. No one else had the same relationship with that person that you had. Two of you may have been sisters—or brothers, or parents—to the one who died, but each of you had a different relationship with that person. And each of you experience grief in a different way.

"Third, I strongly encourage you to give up the idea that there is a fixed time frame for mourning. Unfortunately (or perhaps fortunately) human emotions don't operate by clocks or calendars. The length and depth of your mourning will depend on the nature of your relationship with the loved one. It may be determined by the amount of time you spent with that person—or perhaps by the quality of time you spent with him or her.

"So, the things that help the grieving process are: talk about your grief with someone who will listen supportively; don't compare your grieving to the way someone else grieves; give up the idea that there is a fixed time when you should arrive at point B in your grieving.

"Now. It's your turn. I want you to share with me and the other people here tonight: What has been most helpful to you in your grieving process? What has someone done or said that helped you most? Remember, there is no required participation. Just share what you want to share—what you think might be helpful to other people."

For about a minute no one spoke. Karen waited.

Vesta Cantrell spoke first. Vesta is a tiny little lady; the number 80 probably represents her age and her weight. She wears no makeup and pulls her hair back into a tight ball on her neck. I see her occasionally (when I'm out early enough) walking her daily two miles first thing in the morning. She is always dressed just as she is tonight—tennis shoes, socks and a shirt-waist dress with a gathered skirt. When it's chilly like tonight, she tops the ensemble with a sweater. We handled her brother's funeral a couple of years ago, and it was one of those where the minister left some doubt about the destination of her brother's soul.

"The night before my brother died," Vesta said, "I asked him to pray the sinner's prayer of repentance with me. He wasn't sick or anything. I wasn't expecting him to die. I just wanted to be sure he was saved. But he refused. I went home and prayed for him. The next morning, my sister-in-law called and said he passed away in the night. Massive coronary. I went to church the next day with a heavy burden. Somebody asked me to sing a solo for the worship service, and I thought I just couldn't. But I decided to ask the Lord to help me, and I got through it. After the service, a man came up to me and said, 'I got a message while you were singing. Your brother is with the Lord.'

"It was like a big burden was lifted from my shoulders. I felt at peace about him."

Karen nodded, but didn't say anything.

Mr. Everett spoke up. He had been my high school principal. He was a small man, but he always had this presence about him. He commanded attention even though he was mild mannered and rarely raised his voice. He had a little less hair than I remembered, and more of it was gray rather than dark brown; but otherwise he looked like he did when I was walking the halls of Hilltop High.

"Katie and I had 27 years together. We married late. She was the librarian at the school where I was the principal. We were both old maids."

Everybody smiled, and a few people laughed.

"We had a good life together, then she got lymphoma and died. At first all I could think about was what I hadn't done, or hadn't said, that I wished I had said. Then a friend, who is here tonight, told me, 'Think about all the good times you had together. Get out those videos you made at Christmas. Write down the good memories. The funny things she said.' I've been doing that ever since, and I've just about worn out those videos. I've got two notebooks full of memories I've written down."

A few other people spoke, and then Mr. Phillips started to speak. His voice broke, and he apologized. Then he took a deep breath. He unfolded a piece of paper he had taken from his pocket.

"The thing that helped me most was this poem that Darrel Bledsoe sent me after Terry died."

(Darrel is a second stringer on the high school basketball team.)

Then he read a poem by A. E. Housman:.

To An Athlete Dying Young

The time you won your town the race,
We chaired you through the market place;
Man and boy stood cheering by,
And home we brought you shoulder-high.

Today, the road all runners come,
Shoulder-high we bring you home,
And set you at your threshold down
Townsman of a stiller town.

Smart lad, to slip betimes away
From fields where glory does not stay
And early though the laurel grows
It withers quicker than the rose.

Eyes the shady night has shut

Cannot see the record cut,
And silence sounds no worse than cheers
After earth has shut the ears:

Now you will not swell the rout
Of lads that wore their honors out,
Runners whom renown outran
And the name died before the man."

When he started reading, I was afraid he would break down before he finished. But as he read, his voice became stronger, and he finished on a firm note, then looked around at the group who had hung on every word.

I had not thought about that poem since high school, and then I had considered it rather cynical. I don't think I would have found it comforting, but I was glad it had helped Mr. P. You never know what's going to be meaningful for a person.

"Terry's in a better place," Mr. Phillips said. "That don't make it any easier for us that are left here, but he had a good life. We have a lot to be thankful for."

Molly had reached for Mrs. Phillips' hand and was holding it tightly.

There were several minutes of silence before Karen asked, "Would anyone like to respond to that or share something that you have found helpful in coping?"

Practically everyone in the room shared something that had made their grieving process a little easier.

When the group ended I was exhausted; but I knew that most of these people would sleep better tonight for having been here.

Anne Russ and Nancy Russ

CHAPTER 22

Bill and Karen, Jim Pat, and I had planned to go to Haven Friday night for dinner and a movie. Karen called about 10 a.m. and said she needed to go a little early to visit one of her members who was in the hospital. She suggested the two of us go together and have Bill and Jim Pat meet us at the restaurant.

On the drive over, Karen updated me about Rebekah. I've known about the family for as long as I can remember. Her parents, Dr. Jim and Elizabeth Prine, own a nursing home in Haven, and it has a reputation as the best in the state. Every patient (even the ones on Medicaid) who wants it has a private room. Every room has a window with a view of the grounds that come close to being as pretty as the garden that is my Dad's pride and joy. Rebekah's mother is the administrator, and Dr. Prine is the doctor for most of the patients in addition to his private geriatric practice.

Rebekah is their only child. I don't know her very well, but she is her parents' child. She is active in politics and plays a major role in the county's Democratic Central Committee. She married Jon Bennett, who manages his parents' car dealership in Hilltop, four or five years ago. They have a two-year-old daughter. I was shocked when Karen told me that Rebekah has been diagnosed with cancer, and it is in an advanced stage. She has been to Houston for treatments, but chose to come back to Haven to be near her family for the remainder of what may be her short life.

When we got to Rebekah's room, she was sitting in a chair near the window. She was expecting Karen but seemed glad to see me too. I found it hard to believe that this tall, beautiful athletic-looking young woman is seriously ill. It is true that her skin has a sickly pallor about it, but her big brown eyes sparkle beneath those dark eyebrows. I remember her having beautiful dark hair, and I realize that the turban she's wearing is probably covering a bald head.

I saw again what I have observed so many times. Karen's presence seems to have a healing effect on people. Rebekah laughed and talked so cheerfully that if she had not looked so frail no one would have known she was ill.

Karen led us all in prayer.

"Creator God, bless Rebekah as she struggles with this illness. Give her the strength and faith to continue her fight. Bless her family, too, as they struggle with her. More than ever, God, your child Rebekah needs to feel your presence. Help her to know and feel that you are with her, right beside her, through every step of this journey. Hold her in the palm of your hand. We thank you, Lord, for her life and her gifts and her presence in our lives. We pray all of these things in the name of your Son, Jesus Christ. Amen."

Karen is so much better at these things than I am. I would have prayed. "Alright, God. This is not fair. Fix it. Make her better right now!" I guess that's why Karen is the priest and I have my own role.

When we started to go, Rebekah said, "I'm glad you came, Lu. I was going to give this to Karen, but since you're here, I'll just give it to you."

She handed me a typed sheet of paper. When I looked at it, she must have read the expression on my face.

"It's my obituary," she said. I wrote it because I wanted Jon and Libby to remember me the way I want to be remembered. A couple of my best friends added to it, and I decided to keep their additions. Put it up, and when the time comes send it to the *Haven Herald*, the *Hilltop Record* and the *Arkansas Gazette*. It's about who I really am, not about a wife and mother who died too young.

"Now don't go looking at me like that," she scolded us. "I'm not giving up just yet. And I won't give up. I'm not leaving my daughter without a fight. I've been approved for some experimental new treatment that may prolong my life. I'm just trying to get all my ducks in a row and be realistic about all this."

There was not a trace of bitterness or anger in Rebekah's voice. Her face looked determined, but her eyes were sad. No matter how much faith someone has, it must be horrible to think about leaving a child behind. I wondered if Rebekah didn't beat this illness if her daughter would think she had been abandoned. How long would it be before Libby would realize what really happened and how her mother would have given anything to be there while she was growing up. I offered up my own silent prayer of "Fix this now!" to God. I hoped He or She or Somebody was listening.

When we got in the car, I read the obituary to Karen.

Rebekah Prine Bennett passed away _____
_____. She is survived by her husband, Jonathan
Bennett; her 20-month- old daughter, Elizabeth Prine
Bennett; her parents, James and Elizabeth Cotham Bennett;
and her dog, Pedro. She was 34.

Rebekah graduated from Haven High School and got a
BA in Political Science from Yale. She finished a law
degree at Harvard and for a short time practiced corporate
law. However, she quickly decided that she was about as
comfortable with corporate law as she had been in the only
bikini she ever owned. So she left the law firm and set out
to explore the world she had read about in Shirley
McClain's autobiographies.

On a 10-day trek in the Himalayas, she met the love of
her life, Jonathan Bennett, an adventurer in his own right. It
didn't take long for Rebekah to realize she had found a soul
mate, and she followed Jon to the rain forest of Ecuador
where he proposed. They married a year after they met and
Elizabeth was born a year later. Rebekah had "found
herself" in the starring role of Loving Wife and Mother.

After Elizabeth was born, they moved to Washington,
D.C., where Rebekah worked for a Democratic Senator
until the Republicans voted her out of a job. The couple
then moved to Hilltop where Rebekah continued to do life
the only way she knew—with all her heart.

Rebekah's wide range of interests attracted friends of
all ages and backgrounds. She read everything from
mysteries and novels to biographies and books on
spirituality. Her appetite for knowledge was insatiable. She
loved dancing, singing, listening to music, sailing, walking
on the beach and hiking mountain trails. She was one of
those rare people who really appreciates and enjoys
teenagers and was a perennial sponsor of the Youth
Fellowship at St. Luke's Episcopal Church.

Her favorite pastimes included playing with her
daughter and enjoying the gourmet meals Jon loves to
cook. She will be remembered for her sense of humor,
enthusiasm for life, and her ability to relate to people—

from infants to the elderly—with warmth and a total lack of pretension.

A celebration of Rebekah's life will be held at St. Luke's Episcopal Church. In lieu of flowers, please send contributions to Boys and Girls Club in Hilltop, St. Luke's Youth Fellowship or the Sierra Club.

If I had not looked at Karen when I finished, I would not have known she was responding. Tears were streaming silently down her face. Neither of us said a word as we drove to the restaurant.

When we got to The Catfish Hole, I was relieved to see that Jim Pat and Bill were already there. They stood up when we got to the table, and Bill put his arm around Karen's shoulder. She had freshened up in the car, but he could tell the visit to Rebekah had really taken it out of her. I realized how important it must be for Karen to have Bill for support. He works for the state parks service and has what he calls a "low stress job." He loves the outdoors and that's where he spends most of his days. His laid back occupation must provide a nice balance to her emotionally charged one. I wondered for a moment what it would be like not to have Jim Pat in my life. I reached for his hand and squeezed it as we sat down.

The Catfish Hole, in my opinion has the best fish in the area. Whatever they roll it in before frying, it's seasoned just right—not too salty, but just enough that you don't have to add to it. We all ordered the same thing. Fried catfish steaks with French fries, cole slaw and hushpuppies, and iced tea. I don't know about the others, but the term soul food had real meaning for me right now. The waitress brought a bowl of pickled green tomatoes and sliced onions for "appetizers."

I ate all my fish and the last piece of Jim Pat's—and, following my example, Bill ate the last piece off Karen's plate. I may not want catfish again for three months, but when I am hungry for catfish, I like lots of it.

CHAPTER 23

I had suggested we see the movie *Waking Ned Devine*. The rest of the group was surprised that I would choose a movie about a funeral, but I had read the reviews that suggested it was funny. Besides, it was set in Ireland, and I was looking forward to the beautiful scenery. Ireland is high on my list of about 100 places I'd like to visit some day.

The ticket line wasn't long, and I spotted a familiar face up ahead. I walked up to speak to Harley before I realized that his companion was Janice. Finally! Someone who takes my advice!

I thought I spoke nonchalantly, but Janice said, "Thanks, Lu. Harley told me you encouraged him to ask me out."

We both laughed, and I gave Harley a thumbs-up before returning to my place in line.

The movie would have been worth seeing just for the scenery and one hilarious scene. The picture of an old skinny man riding a motorcycle while wearing nothing but a helmet may not strike some people as funny, but I could tell from the laughter in the theatre that I was not the only one who appreciated it. Jim Pat laughed quietly, but Bill roared.

The movie is set in a small village in Ireland where everybody in town buys lottery tickets for the six million dollar pot. Fortunately one of them—Ned Devine—wins. Unfortunately, when he hears the news on television, he has a heart attack and dies. Now the trick is for the whole town to keep the secret, bury Ned, have an imposter pose as Ned and divvy up the lottery among the 56 citizens of the town. When the lottery representative shows up just as they are having Ned's funeral, they decide to substitute another name for Ned's. Thus, the imposter gets to attend his own funeral. And his best friend eulogizes him, saying, "I'm sorry I never told old Fred what a great friend he was."

A lone dissenter in the town and the revelation to a few people that Ned has an heir threaten to blow the whole thing, but this being a "happily ever after" movie, everything works out. It was just the kind of break I needed.

After the movie, we stopped at a soda shop that has a 50's theme. It has an authentic juke box and a karaoke machine, and it was crowded with teenagers. Considering all I had eaten for dinner, I should have just had a diet Coke, but I happened to know that their apple pie is to die for. Who knew when I would be back again? Life is too short to pass up good pie. Bill agreed to order some just to keep me company, and when the waitress asked if we wanted ice cream on it, we both nodded.

Jim Pat brought up the movie.

"Maybe it would be a good idea to have funerals before people die," he said. "People generally don't say negative things at funerals, and some people never get to hear all the good things people think about them."

Bill said, "I read this week where a man in Wisconsin did just that. He decided he wanted to direct his own funeral. So he bought the coffin, paid for everything including the burial plot, and had a funeral service, with a closed casket, of course. He chose all the music, some of it not very funeral-like, and all his friends had a chance to say whatever they wanted to say. After the service, they returned the coffin to the funeral home until further notice, and the man and his friends all had a big party. He says when he dies they can just bury the body. He's already had the funeral."

I didn't say it out loud, but I kind of hope that idea doesn't catch on around here. I don't want to get into the business of renting out caskets for pre-funeral services.

Karen said, "As long as we're telling funeral stories...just bear with us, Lu. The priest that I did my internship with in seminary used to tell this story for the truth.

"Apparently a member of his parish who was an old curmudgeon passed away. Reverend Johnson even admitted that this man—a Mr. Ryan, I believe—was the kind of parishioner who was hard to love. Anyway, Ryan was a wealthy man and employed about half the community, so people showed up out of some sense of duty or maybe even respect. Some kind hearted soul got up to eulogize the man and went on and on about what a generous, loving, and honest man Mr. Ryan had been. After it was over, an employee of Ryan's came up to Reverend Johnson and asked if he could look in the casket. The Reverend thought this man was especially close to Ryan and needed to see the body for some sort of closure. He told the man it was highly unusual, but perhaps it could be worked out.

"'Why is it you feel the need to actually see the body?' he asked. The man didn't even pause. 'The Ryan I knew was a real jerk. After that eulogy, I just wanted to check and see if I came to the right service.'"

Bill and I smiled at the joke, but for some reason it struck Jim Pat as being absolutely hysterical. He laughed so hard that he spit cola all over the table, and then turned red from embarrassment over his outburst.

"I'm sorry," he said. "But that just tickled me. I've been to funerals where I've felt the same way. Although I guess it's nice to think that no matter how bad we screw up in life, when we die, folks will only remember the good things. "

Anne Russ and Nancy Russ

CHAPTER 24

Wouldn't you know it? Right in the middle of enjoying a humdinger of a mid-life crisis, Jim Pat's Uncle Whit up and has a fatal heart attack. Just three weeks into a New Year, Whit keeled over right in the middle of a business lunch at The Club Car. They called 911, but he was gone by the time the paramedics arrived.

It was pretty awful for Jim Pat and his family. The last words Whit had heard from any of his family were all unkind. Sure, Carlene was the one trying to make off with the family heirlooms and threatening to sell off the family business, but they blamed all of it on Whit. They all liked Carlene and were pretty annoyed, not to mention embarrassed, that one of their own could leave his partner of 35 years for a woman who on the day of their wedding had yet to be born.

So they were all mad as hell at Whit when he died—and they were even madder that he went and did it while they were all so mad at him! At least that's the way Jim Pat articulated the situation to me.

The funeral—from a purely logistical standpoint—should have been a piece of cake. Whit and Carlene had pre-planned everything years ago and had paid in full everything right down to side-by-side grave plots. Easy as pie (to continue with my pastry metaphors)— except for the fact that Whit and his wife had been in the process of divorcing when the skirt chaser met his maker. Notice I said process. The divorce was not yet final, and no changes had been made to the plans. I was a little anxious to see how this cookie would crumble.

I spent most of the afternoon over at Jim Pat's house with the rest of the family—including Carlene. She told me that she and Jim Pat's mom, Nancy, would be handling all the arrangements. I generally have an excellent poker face, but it must have slipped this time, because she added, "I know everyone knows what's been going on for the past few months, but he was my husband for 35 years. I feel I owe him this much."

We made arrangements for the two of them to come to the funeral home first thing the next morning.

As she walked away to talk to some other family member about the obituary, I couldn't help thinking about what a bizarre range of emotions Carlene Whitney must be experiencing. I mean, here is a man to whom she, by all accounts, was totally devoted for over half her life. Then after he hurts her by cheating and humiliates her by his choice of partner and lack of discretion, he goes and dies. Does she celebrate that the cad who left her high and dry got his? Does she grieve for the man she loved for so long? This is one of those situations in which I offer up a little prayer to God asking to never know the answer to these questions first hand.

After a few hours, Jim Pat grabbed my hand and said, "I've got to get out of here. Let's go grab dinner at the Club Car."

Obviously, the grief had caused his faculties to take a brief recess from his brain.

"Are you out of your mind?" I hissed at him in a low voice. "You are Whit's nephew. I am your girlfriend and the local funeral director. We live in a small town. Don't you think it would seem a little odd for us to be having an intimate dinner in the very restaurant where your uncle keeled over not six hours before?"

"Okay, okay," he agreed. "But can we go to your place and order pizza? I cannot endure another morbid mourner coming to pay his respects."

The house was starting to fill up. Because Whit passed away in such a public place, word of his untimely demise spread quickly. The food was already starting to arrive. So far I counted three casseroles and two cobblers. I had sampled both the latter and the peach was far superior to the apple.

"Should we say something to your mom?" I asked.

"I already told her I'd probably cut out. Dad and Carlene are here. She's doing fine, considering."

Jim Pat hadn't really said much the entire afternoon, but he began to make up for lost time on the ride over to my place.

"I feel really bad that I don't feel worse," Jim Pat confessed to me. "When I was a little kid, I used to think my Uncle Whit was the greatest thing ever. He was almost like a second Dad. He took me to my first major league baseball game. He showed me how to manage my first bank account. He even taught me how to drive—it made Mom and Dad too nervous to get in the car with me.

"But in the last few years, he changed. Since I came back here after pharmacy school, I bet he hasn't spent more than an hour with me outside of 'official' family gatherings. Our family has plenty of money, but Uncle Whit became obsessed with making more and more. The only thing he cared about more than money was control—which was why he didn't want to sell the bank for any price. And then the thing with Aunt Carlene—how could he do that to her? Not only did he screw himself up, he turned my Pollyanna aunt into a bitter, mean woman.

"I'm not glad that he died, but I can't get all torn up about the fact that he's dead. There. Am I awful?"

I had to bite back a giggle. Here is a man whose face still holds glimpses of the Howdy-Doody-look-a-like boy he once was asking me if he is awful. It really was humorous, but the guy was serious, so I answered him just as seriously.

"No, you're not awful," I assured him. "Don't you know that there is no way you *should* feel after someone dies except for the way you feel? Have you picked up no "dealing with death" vibes the whole time we've been dating? So you're not that upset right now. That's right now. I bet you'll shed some tears before all is said and done; but if you don't, that's okay, too."

"Sure," he said. Then he suddenly switched gears.

"I think it's safe to say that of the two of us, I have had the worse day. Wouldn't you agree?"

"Yes..." I said tentatively, wondering where he was going with this.

"Since I've been through such an ordeal," he continued. "I believe it's only fair that I pick the pizza we order."

I groaned, because I knew what was coming.

"Ham and pineapple with extra cheese. You can pick off the pineapple."

True enough, but there's no getting around the juice those little tidbits leave behind. They soak the whole pie.

Anne Russ and Nancy Russ

CHAPTER 25

The next day started early with an eight o'clock meeting with Jim Pat's mom and his Aunt Carlene. We met in Grandpa's office. Grandpa had made a pot of coffee for everyone, and I had picked up some really fabulous apple cranberry muffins. Normally we don't cater a funeral planning, but we thought this one might be a little tense. And I always think food can help calm any situation. After Grandpa and I expressed our condolences, we got right down to business.

"Just keep everything as we planned it," Carlene started right in. "I would like to have the funeral as soon as possible. Could we have the visitation today?"

"Now, Carlene," Nancy said softly. "I know this can't be easy for you, but nothing has even been run in the paper. No one will know to come. Why don't we schedule it for tomorrow and the funeral for the day after that? That way we can get it to the paper today for tomorrow's edition. That is, if Gibbs can accommodate us."

Both Nancy and Carlene were extremely calm and rational for two women who had just lost a brother and an almost-ex husband. Grandpa gave me a sideways glance. We had both seen this before. A lot of people handle the funeral part of a death quite well. As long as there are plans to be made and things to be taken care of, they don't have to really think about what has happened. Though Grandpa and I find this stage of the grief process fairly predictable, what we can't predict is when it will end. No doubt Nancy and Carlene will each break down and grieve in their own way, but when and where that will happen is anybody's guess.

"That will be fine," Grandpa assured them. "We'll set up the visitation room for tomorrow evening. I've already talked to Brother Toomey, and we tentatively scheduled the funeral for 10 a.m. on Thursday...if that meets with your approval."

Grandpa has this wonderfully soothing tone about his voice. Surely 70 years in the funeral business has helped to fine tune the calming effect of his voice, but a sound like that isn't something you learn—it's a gift you have to be born with.

Both women nodded. We were just about to wrap everything up, when the door burst open. Everyone in the room jumped and turned to look at the entryway. There stood a wild-looking, red-eyed Tiffany.

Tiffany's corkscrew-curled blond bob looked like she'd stuck her finger in a light socket. Without any make-up she was still pretty, but the lack of paint made her look even younger than her 25 years. The bright red paint on her inordinately long nails was chipping. Instead of her usual tight jeans and cleavage-revealing tops, she was wearing a faded sweat suit with a "What Me Worry?" legend across the chest. She looked like a pitiful child who had awakened in the middle of the night to a crisis.

"What have you done with him?" she screamed. "Where is he? What have you done?"

Everyone was so stunned that nobody, even Grandpa, could reply to her questions.

"Do you know how I found out he was dead?" she demanded. "Do you? I stopped at the pharmacy to pick up some hair color yesterday afternoon. When it was closed I asked Don, the barber next door, what was up. He told me the place was closed because the owner's brother had died. That's how I found out."

"Of course," Carlene sneered. "I can't imagine why I didn't think to notify you. All the women my husband was sleeping with should have been at the top of my list."

I glanced at Grandpa. He looked at me. We both knew what was coming. Cat fight.

"How dare you talk down to me," Tiffany said. "If you had kept him happy at home, he never would have come looking for me. He did, you know. Don't blame me for breaking up your marriage. Your husband tried to pick me up in a bar. I wouldn't give him the time of day. It took two months of flowers, jewelry and clothes for me to even agree to go out with him. He came looking for me, baby!"

Carlene had turned quite pale.

"Tiffany," I interjected. "This is really not the place to hash all this out. Why don't we go into my office and discuss the situation."

"Not the place?" she screamed. "My man is laying on a cold slab somewhere in this meat market because of HER! She did this to him. She was going to bleed him dry in the divorce—take his house, his bank, everything. He couldn't take it. The stress killed him. SHE killed him!"

Grandpa, who always knows what to do in a difficult client situation, just sat at the conference table with his mouth hanging open. I was considering calling the police when Carlene rallied.

"How dare you come here," she started in a small voice. "How dare you come here to disgrace the name of a man I gave my life to for longer than you've been alive."

Her voice got louder.

"Surely you know that you were just a distraction. If Whit were still here, your days would be numbered. Surely you know that he would never give up his home, his business and his family for a little bleached blonde bimbo in pedal pushers and a push-up bra!"

I had no idea Carlene could be so eloquent. I thought Tiffany's head was going to explode. Grandpa and I just sat there to see what would happen next.

"Stop it! Both of you just stop it!"

I had forgotten Nancy was there.

"My only brother is dead," she sobbed. "And thanks to the two of you, all anyone will remember about him is that he was running around with some girl young enough to be his daughter and that his wife was going to take him for all he was worth. I hope you're both very happy!"

With that she got up and stormed out of the office, leaving Tiffany, Carlene, Grandpa and me staring after her, stupefied.

At that point, I once again suggested to Tiffany, "Why don't we go into my office and talk?"

This time, she assented.

While Grandpa and Carlene finished up the nuts and bolts of the esteemed Mr. Whitley's funeral, Tiffany sank into my couch and began sobbing. I sat in the chair opposite her, vaguely aware of the contrast in our sizes.

"How could this happen?" she cried. "How could he die on me? And that witch is controlling his funeral. Don't I have a say about it?"

I was trying to work up some compassion for this woman. I understood she lost someone—it appeared that she really did love him. But I have very little patience with people who cheat on their spouses and for the persons who cheat with them. I felt badly for letting my personal feelings affect my professional life. No matter how I felt about Tiffany whatever-her-last-name-was, she had lost a loved one who was now in our care. And that made her a client—sort of.

"I'm very sorry for your loss," I told her truthfully, in my best professional voice. "I realize that you would like to be a part of this funeral service and have some input into it. However, he was still married to, and not even legally separated from, his wife when he passed from this world. Mr. Whitley pre-planned all the details of his funeral and his burial. Though he may have changed his mind about part, or all, of the original plan, he failed to let anyone at Gibbs know in written or verbal communication. Therefore we cannot legally alter the stipulations set forth in the contract."

I don't know whether that last part is true—about the legality of changing the plans—but I knew she wouldn't know enough to contradict me. Even with that little white lie, I had been courteous, clear and sympathetic. No one could question the professionalism of the way I handled the situation.

"So you're saying that I have no authority in this matter whatsoever?" she finally asked.

"No, I'm sorry, but you don't."

She sat there for a moment looking pensive. Then a look of panic swept across her face. She stood and screamed, "Oh, my God, no!"

"Look," I said. "I really am very sorry. If you have anything you would like said or done at the funeral, perhaps I can make some suggestions to the family."

"Screw the funeral," she spat out. "He hated his wife. There's no way he wanted to be buried next to her for all eternity. But if he didn't even bother to change his burial arrangements, whaddaya wanna bet the lazy, good for nothing, son of a bitch didn't get around to changing his will either. I'm gonna be stuck with a big fat nothing!"

The time for professionalism had passed. I had given this woman the benefit of the doubt—I believed she was truly distraught over the death of the man she had been sleeping with. Actually, she was distraught, but for reasons I found reprehensible. (Sorry, I can get on a moral high horse from time to time). With her final remarks, my efforts at remaining impartial had flown out the window.

I stood up.

"I think you better leave now," I told her.

"Sure," she said, not picking up on the tone of my voice. "I just need to make a couple of phone calls. Can I use your office?"

She was standing now, and I looked down at her.

"Perhaps you didn't understand," I said through clenched teeth. "Get out of my office, right NOW!

Tiffany may not be all that bright, but she's no dummy. She high tailed it out of my office quicker than a jackrabbit on steroids.

When I went back into Grandpa's office, Carlene had gone home.

"In 70 years, I thought I'd seen it all," Grandpa said. "But that was a first for me. There was that one man who had a coronary in his mistress's bed, but that was back in the 40s. The mistress had the good sense not to show her face, and the wife pretended it never happened. She told everyone he died gardening in the back yard, and she bribed the ambulance drivers who hauled him out of his lover's bed to tell the same story."

"How did you find out what really happened?"

"Well, the mistress was actually a professional, if you know what I mean. After this guy's heart attack, she decided that it was a sign from God that what she was doing was a sin. She'd piled up quite a bit of money by this time, and made a few lucrative post-war investments—GE stock mainly, and she dedicated the rest of her life to the service of others. Sometime in the early seventies, she got a little tipsy at Doc Green's Christmas Party and spilled the beans to me."

Grandpa paused for effect. "You know, Miss Mattie never could keep a secret."

If he was trying to shock me, it worked.

Anne Russ and Nancy Russ

CHAPTER 26

Whit's funeral went off without any of the dramatics that preceded it. Tiffany had the good sense not to show—I guess she found out that the will had indeed not been amended—and Nancy and Carlene seemed to have come to a truce. Grandpa handled the funeral so I could sit with Jim Pat and the rest of the family during the service. And Jim Pat did cry—not for the man who cheated on his wife and embarrassed his family, but for the man who took him to Cardinals games and taught him how to drive a stick shift. I guess he was right—when we die, the ones who love us tend to hold on to the good things we managed to do during life.

The rest of winter was relatively uneventful. We did have a big snow in early March (here that means about three inches), followed by an ice storm, and everything just about shut down for a week. Grandpa, Mo and I were thankful no one decided to die that week because it would have been almost impossible to get the body, have the relatives in to do planning, and hold a funeral. And even if we could have gotten all of that done, the ground was too hard to dig a grave.

Though there were a few funerals over the winter after the bad weather cleared, business didn't get interesting again until Joanne Greenfield finally passed away in early April. I say "finally" like she was an old woman or something. In fact, she was only 64; but she had been chronically ill for a long time—something to do with diabetes complications. It seemed she had been on the brink of death nearly all my life.

So, here's the thing. Mr. Greenfield passed from this world in a most untimely manner over 20 years ago when a produce truck had a blowout right in front of his house at the exact time he was at the end of the drive checking the mail. Doctors said he never knew what hit him. He died the instant the truck plowed him over. The driver, who was based out of Memphis, was not physically injured, but people say he never got over what happened.

Mrs. Greenfield played the lonely widow for years. She really loved her husband, and she nearly wasted away pining after him in that big old house. It was ages before she could go to the mailbox without bursting into tears. Sometimes the mail would be overflowing because she just couldn't bear to retrieve it. Lord knows why she didn't just move, but she insisted on keeping everything—the house, the yard, and even the adjoining vacant lot they owned just as it was when her Eddie was living.

Her son and daughter-in-law lived right next door with their three sons, one of whom was my budding young historian—Casey.

About 10 years after Mr. Greenfield died, an itinerant handy man came through town and Mrs. Greenfield hired him to do some work for her. He didn't have a place to live, and Mrs. G's house was much too big for one person, so Mark Abercrombie moved in with her. Boy, did that set the town to talking! Not only were they not married; Mark was at least 25 years younger than she. He was still there 10 years later when Joanne died.

I met Mark one summer when I was home from college. I thought he was kind of romantic. He had been everywhere. At the time, he was just shy of 30; and he had already spent a year on the island of Nantucket, worked four ski seasons in Colorado, studied art and architecture at three different colleges (never did get a degree), hiked the Appalachian trail, and hitch hiked all the way to Alaska repairing whatever needed to be fixed along the way for pocket money. He happened through Hilltop about the time that Joanne Greenfield realized that a house minus a "honey-do" for 10 years was in sore need of repairs.

At the time, Murphy Brown was a popular sitcom. It was like life imitating art (if you're willing to include television in the art category). Remember that painter, Eldon, who came to do one project and ended up staying forever? Well, that's kind of what Mark Abercrombie did—only he didn't go home at night. He definitely earned his keep. The house must be worth a fortune now. It was originally built just after World War One. Mark restored the entire house right down to the crown moldings.

But historically accurate restoration was the last thing anyone mentioned when they talked about the Greenfield home. Nobody knew exactly what was going on there, except that Mark Abercrombie was totally devoted to Mrs. Greenfield.

"There has to be something going on between them," Aunt Lettie used to say. "Every single woman in town has made a play for him, and he's not even remotely interested. Besides that, he's far too rugged looking to be gay."

Even when Mrs. Greenfield got sick, Mark stayed. Jim Pat told me he used to come in the pharmacy for her medicine all the time. He even learned to give her insulin shots. I always wondered why he stayed. Maybe he had packed enough adventure into his life at an early age and just wanted to be settled for awhile.

Now the younger Mrs. Greenfield, Joanne's daughter-in-law Clara Beth, did not look upon this situation favorably. Clara Beth is the secretary at the Methodist church (whose door I darken from time to time), and she viewed the entire arrangement as extremely unseemly. She didn't feel that someone in her position—on a church staff and all—should have a relative (by blood or marriage) who was living in sin. I hate that term. I believe if Clara Beth would actually consult her Bible instead of simply thumping it, she would learn that we were all sinners (hey, I read my own Bible from time to time!). If sweet, little frail Mrs. Greenfield is living in sin, then the rest of us (Clara Beth included!) must be positively mired in it!

Clara Beth actually forbade her three young sons to visit their grandmother in "that house" as she always referred to her mother-in-law's home. And she always said it with a look that made you suspect that she had just caught a whiff of some terribly troubling smell.

I knew that at least one of the Greenfield grandsons slipped over to see his granny almost every day. My Chester A. Arthur scholar, Casey, was Joanne's youngest grandson, and he thought his grandma was indeed the grandest thing around. I guess every kid has to rebel a little, and Casey was getting his in by sneaking over to that "den of iniquity" (I swear I heard Clara Beth call it that one day in the aisle at Piggly Wiggly) to have milk and cookies.

Knowing how Clara Beth felt about Mark, I was not looking forward to the visitation. People are uncomfortable enough in that little room with a person without having family tensions add to the trauma. Something about the solemnity of death just doesn't sit well with hatred and resentment in the air. But then very few things sit well with hatred and resentment in the air.

I remember when Arlo Trichell died, right after I came to work for Grandpa. Arlo had been married to Miz Ida for over 30 years, when one day she just keeled over into her prize-winning begonias and died. I believe it was some sort of aneurysm. Ida was one of those saints whose presence blesses the world from time to time. I know folks always say wonderful things about people when they die, but in Miz Ida's case, they were all true. I bet she had done something good for just about every man, woman and child in Hilltop, and most of the pets, too. Ida just loved animals. She also made a to-die-for chicken and broccoli casserole that no one has yet to duplicate.

Poor Arlo was just struck dumb with grief when she died. He really was just a wreck. Their three kids were all grown, and he was left all alone. Well, lo and behold if he didn't show up six months to the day after the funeral married to a woman from Paragould whom he had met at a regional meeting of the Optimist Club. The three kids were livid. How could their daddy do that to their mother? And the new wife didn't help matters much. The first thing Patricia did was redecorate the entire house, purging it of all things Ida. And to make matters worse, she changed the family name—the pronunciation, not the spelling. Arlo and his people have been around these parts for years, and they've always been just plain old Trichells (pronounced *tree shells*). But once Patricia came into the picture, all of a sudden she and Arlo are Tri (with a short "I") SHELLS (with emphasis on the shell). It was all people talked about for months.

I have some friends in Louisiana who insist that the Perots there pronounce their name Pea'-row. They think the presidential candidate, Ross Perot, changed it to Pe-row' when he got rich.

Anyway, when Arlo's time came, his visitation was like being at a Hatfield-McCoy wedding. There were two sides to the room—those with the TREEshells and those with the TriSHELLS. Poor Arlo's coffin was the dividing line. I don't stand much on ceremony, but the whole thing bordered on sacrilege.

I was afraid that Joanne Greenfield's visitation would be more of the same.

But it was not to be. Mark Abercrombie didn't even show up.

"Where is Mark?" I whispered to Casey when Clara Beth couldn't hear.

"Not comin'," Casey whispered back, clearly enjoying our secret. Told me he already said goodbye to Gran, and he didn't need to stand around making nice with people."

Abercrombie didn't show up for the funeral either. Miss Mattie told me afterwards he had already left town.

"Ralph down at the post office told me he got on a bus yesterday," she whispered to me before the service began.

Our local post office is also the bus stop in town. Greyhound comes through here once a day.

"All he had with him was a duffel bag. The very same one he rode into town with 10 years ago."

I very much doubted it was indeed the same duffel bag from so many years ago, but Miss Mattie does have a flair for the dramatic, and it did make a good story. I wondered if Casey, or anyone else, knew where Mark had gone. During the funeral I day-dreamed about where that bus would take Mark Abercrombie and whether he was ready to start wandering again.

Anne Russ and Nancy Russ

CHAPTER 27

It was a warm day, even for April, and I went home after the funeral planning to sit on Grandpa's deck and soak up some sunshine. Despite my hair color, I do tan a little and like to get a little color on my face from time to time.

I figured I'd do the afternoon up right and stopped by Dairy Shack to pick up a pineapple-banana shake. Normally, I order the chocolate-peanut butter shake, but I'm trying to adopt some healthier eating habits. I thought maybe the banana-pineapple combination counted for at least one of the five fruits and vegetables I was supposed to eat each day. I think Rosie would count it and probably even give me a bonus for getting enough bone strengthening calcium through the vanilla ice cream. And, of course, I didn't intend to ask my nutritionist boyfriend for his opinion.

Dad's car was in the driveway, which surprised me a little. He usually stays at the bank until after closing time. But it was a beautiful day—too pretty to sit around a bank or a funeral home. I was not surprised to find Dad out in the garden digging in the dirt with such concentration that he didn't even notice that I'd come home. He had a flat of bright colored flowers that included those little yellow button-like things and the ones with the bright waxy-looking leaves and blooms.

What had I been doing lately? The garden was beautiful. I mean, it's always nice, but this year it was incredible. Have I really been so busy that I just haven't seen those gorgeous...what are they now...Callas? I don't remember ever having seen them in any color except white, but here was a brilliant array of yellow and peach-colored lilies against tall hollyhocks that formed a kind of wall around the garden. (Maybe that's why I hadn't noticed the lilies?)

In the center of the garden is the waterfall. Dad started working on that waterfall the summer after Mom left. He used to send me out looking for stones.

"Okay, Lu," he would say. "This trip I need to look for round smooth stones that are smaller than a softball, but bigger than a golf ball."

Another time, the stones would need to be about the size of the knob on the banister that led to the upstairs of our house. I'd take off around the neighborhood collecting stones of various sizes and then we'd polish them in a little tumbler that dad ordered from a catalog. I don't know if he ever really wanted a waterfall or if he was just looking for something to keep me occupied that summer. But all of my rock collecting and polishing was worth the effort. Listening to the soothing sound of the water trickling over the rocks I get why Dad spends so much time here.

The pool is surrounded by a bed of those big lacy Iris that are Dad's pride and joy, then rows of those little yellow flowers and a mixture of small purple, lavender and red flowers. (I've never been big on learning the names of things. I can sit and enjoy the birds and butterflies all day without even wondering about their names.) And I love to look at Dad's flowers, but I've never bothered to learn what each blossom is called—nor am I interested in digging in the dirt to plant seeds. I am more of a "see the finished product" kind of person.

Dad continued to dig intently in the dirt along the walk that winds through the garden. He had not even noticed me.

"Well, hey Lu. Are you playing hooky, too?"

The woman's voice startled me. I realized that I didn't know how long I had been standing there just looking at the garden and sucking on my shake. I turned and saw Glenda Justice standing right behind me.

"Isn't this unbelievable? I had no idea your dad was a master gardener!" she exclaimed. "He sure knows how to keep a secret."

She caught me by surprise, and I guess I didn't answer quickly enough. I was looking at this handsome woman. Her shapely legs were tan against the expensive white shorts. Glints of auburn and gray alternated in the short hair that framed her face, and her green T-shirt made her eyes look as green as the leaves of the garden. She definitely added to the decor.

"I am so glad I found somebody who can advise me about restoring the gardens at my place," she said.

Her voice was almost giddy. Can a 50-something woman be giddy? And over a garden? Well, maybe she was not exactly giddy, but she was definitely gushing. Then it hit me. This woman was flirting! With my Dad! I wasn't quite sure how I felt about that.

I looked at Dad, and he said, "Hi, Lu. Great afternoon, huh?" acting as if it was the most natural thing in the world for him to be planting flowers while a woman, a very attractive woman, gushed over his gardening skills.

Then something else hit me: He didn't have a clue. He probably thought Glenda was really interested in gardening tips. Well, maybe she was, but I'd bet the farm (or at least the milk cow) that she was interested in more than perennials.

"Hi, Dad. Hi Glenda. I just came home to catch a few rays before I go back to work."

"How about lunch tomorrow?" Glenda said. "I finally got my house painted, and I've done some work in the yard. It's going to take a while, but eventually it will look as good as the picture."

I thought, "Maybe there is some hope for Dad yet."

I *said*, "I'd love to. What time?"

CHAPTER 28

I had lots of work to catch up on and I would be taking a long lunch hour, so I got to the office early. Mo was already there, of course. He greeted me at the door of his office.

"I was just going to call you," he said. "There is someone here to see you."

I was surprised. Nobody comes to a funeral home early in the morning. And obviously Mo didn't know the person or persons who were waiting.

I headed for the reception area. Sitting on the sofa was a tall woman who looked vaguely familiar. Her body was a skeleton with skin stretched tightly over it. Her big, round eyes looked like those on "Precious Memories" creatures except that they were accented by deep, dark circles underneath. She held a purse in one hand and a small shopping bag in the other.

"I'm Lu Gibson," I said, and held out my hand.

When she stood, she reminded me of a big bird like a crane. Her hands were bony like the rest of her body, but the nails on her long fingers were perfectly manicured.

"I know who you are, LuLu," she said as she stood up. She held on to both bags so she couldn't shake my hand.

"I used to do your mother's hair when you were just a little girl. And she always brought you with her."

I hope I didn't wince visibly. Most of the time I can forget I had a mother. These reminders that I not only had one (have one?), but that she might even have been a good mother at one time don't sit well with me.

"What can I do for you, Ms...?" I asked. She had not told me her name.

"Edna," she said, "Edna Sanders."

The name sounded familiar. It was beginning to come back to me. I remembered her little shop a few miles out of town where Mom used to go get her hair done. She always gave me colors and a coloring book to keep me occupied. Now I remembered that I always admired those perfectly manicured nails.

The other thing I remembered about her was that she told funny stories. I don't remember any of them, but she always used different voices for all the characters involved. The stories made my mother laugh, and her funny voices kept me entertained. I had forgotten all about Mrs. Sanders. But, then, I had tried to forget everything and everybody associated with my mother.

"Mrs. Sanders," I said now. "I do remember you."

"LuLu, I need a favor. It's a very private affair," she said, looking around her.

My curiosity was piqued.

"I will be glad to help in any way I can," I told her.

Edna took a vase out of the shopping bag. I noticed her hands were shaking.

"This is my Jimmy," she said.

I waited.

"He died a month ago, and I had him cremated. It's going to be hard to give him up, but I want to bury him in our family plot at the Hilltop Cemetery."

"I think that can be arranged," I said. "Are you planning to have a memorial service prior to going to the grave site?"

"I don't want a service." She spoke quickly, becoming more agitated.

"Well, we'd be happy to have one of our staff prepare a plot for the burial."

"No," she said. "I have my shovel in the car. I've checked, and with all the rain we've had recently, the ground is soft enough. I just would like you to go with me in case someone else comes to the cemetery while I'm there."

"All right," I said slowly, trying to figure out what was going on and acting as if this were the most normal request in the world. "When would you like to do it?"

"This morning." And she added, "Now. If that's possible."

"Okay," I said, still very slowly and deliberately, trying to buy some time. "Let me just…"

Just what? Call Grandpa? He's probably having breakfast right now. Talk to Jim Pat? He's not in the funeral business. Think. Think. Think. Smile at the lady. She's already upset enough. Aha! Tell Mo.

"Can you excuse me just a moment? I'll be right back," I said.

I quickly explained the situation to Mo.

"This is too bizarre," I said. "What should I do?"

Mo thought for a moment and then said, "I think you should take her out to the cemetery and help her bury her son."

Mo didn't even have to act like it all made sense to him—it did. Nothing ever surprises that man! He did fill in some more details about Edna for me. Her husband had been an alcoholic and committed suicide when their son was very small. She had worked hard to make a living for the two of them. Her son Jimmy became an actor and moved somewhere out in California, and as soon as he got settled there, he moved his mother out there to be with him. Mo hadn't heard anything about either of them since she had moved.

While interesting enough, no part of this story explained why Edna Sanders was basically sneaking her son's remains into the ground. Mo offered to go with us to the cemetery. But I turned him down, feeling that I ought to be able to handle this situation. Surely at some point my grandfather would actually retire from this business, and I would be on my own. Mo would always be here, but he has his own job to do.

I grabbed my purse and returned to Edna.

"Okay, everything is taken care of." I told her, pretending I had been making arrangements instead of freaking out in the back room. "Are you ready?"

"Ready," she said, and actually smiled.

She insisted on taking her car—a huge 10-year-old Cadillac which she drove like it was the only vehicle on the road. Fortunately, it was still early enough that there was little traffic.

On the way to the cemetery, she talked about Jimmy—what a good actor he was, how handsome he was, but mostly what a good son he had been. Once she got started, she hardly took a breath—and she still imitated the different voices of the players in her tales.

"You know," she said (of course, I didn't), "Jimmy converted to Catholicism. After he got sick, the priest came every day. He performed some kind of ritual every time he came so Jimmy could die with a clean heart, with all his sins forgiven. I'm not Catholic, but it made Jimmy feel better, and that made me feel better. He—the priest—had a great sense of humor. I didn't really know that professional religious people were allowed to be funny! I just love a good joke. It was a sad time, and it helped to have a good laugh occasionally.

"One day, I asked Father Herbert what he thought Heaven would be like.

"He said, 'Well, Edna, whatever you like to do most on earth, you will get to do more of that in Heaven.'

"I said, 'But, Father, what I like to do most on earth is gossip.'"

She waited, and I spoke for the first time since we got in the car.

"And what did he say?" I really wanted to know.

Edna answered, "There was a long pause. And then Father said, 'Well, Edna, you'll just have to take that up with the Lord.'"

Edna laughed loudly and slapped the steering wheel. I gripped the dashboard while saying a silent prayer of thanks that there was no traffic coming toward us as her big boat of a car swerved into the wrong lane.

At the cemetery, I dug a hole in the plot next to the double plot where Edna and her husband's names were on the marker. I have presided over many graveside services, but this was the first time I have actually dug a hole for burial. It was kind of eerie, yet powerful all at the same time. Edna placed the vase in the hole, and I replaced the dirt. There were no flowers. I figured the flowers and a marker would come later.

Edna said, "Goodbye Jimmy. You were a wonderful son. I love you."

I was sure Grandpa would say something appropriate at this time, but since I couldn't think of anything appropriate, I put my arms around Edna. She buried her face in my hair, and I could feel her whole body shaking as she sobbed.

After a few minutes I offered to drive her back to the office, and she handed me the keys.

Somewhere between the slightly scary drive to the cemetery and the process of laying Jimmy to rest, it dawned on me how Jimmy must have died. As I drove Mrs. Sanders back to the funeral home, I thought about how tragic it was that this woman not only lost her son, she didn't even feel she could invite her friends to grieve with her. Obviously, the cause of Jimmy's death was something she couldn't bring herself to express. And yet, she had clearly forgiven him for any embarrassment or pain his lifestyle had caused her.

Back at the office Edna thanked me profusely, calling me her "little LuLu," and drove off, seemingly in a much better frame of mind.

After that experience, the prospect of having lunch with Glenda sounded better and better. I called and asked if I could come early, and she assured me she would be happy to have me.

The beautiful old house sparkled, and the manicured lawn with its banks of azaleas bushes and beds of variegated annuals lifted my spirits.

Glenda met me at the door.

"Come on in and have a glass of iced tea while I finish up the salad."

As I walked through the front room, I remembered that Glenda had told me she had a "flair for design." The house was a showplace. I sat down in the cozy little room just off the kitchen while she got the tea. The mantle was lined with photographs. There was one of Wendell, in his younger days, and another showed a couple that was obviously their parents. (The woman strongly resembled Glenda, but her clothes hinted of a different era.) One picture was a handsome black man holding up a big fish. In another picture, an older version of the same man was standing on the prow of a nice fishing boat.

I was still looking at the picture when Glenda came in with the tea.

"Now you know why I didn't come back to Hilltop," she said.

I looked at her, not understanding.

"That's Charlie," she said, nodding at the picture.

Charlie was her husband. Charlie was black. Though it's getting better, Hilltop has a long history of segregation. Glenda had not felt free to bring her husband, whom she obviously loved very much, to meet her family and friends.

A little too much revelation for one day. It was the second time in a few hours that I was hit upside the head with how unjust the world can be. I was more than ready for the hearty dish of pasta topped with green beans, smoked turkey sausage and stewed tomatoes that Glenda set before me. Food never solved anything, but it can sure help sometimes.

Anne Russ and Nancy Russ

CHAPTER 29

Now as much as I like to have my finger on the pulse of Hilltop, I'm not one to use what I know to hurt anyone. I like to collect juicy tidbits of information, but I rarely offer any up, and I certainly never intentionally use my knowledge for personal gain or to conjure up any ill will. But sometimes, you just gotta use what you know to do what's right.

When I had to turn on the air conditioning in my car that morning, I knew it was going to be a scorcher. If it's already a little uncomfortable by 8 a.m., you know that by mid-day the heat will be unbearable. I stopped by The Diner to pick up an iced coffee for a cool pick-me-up, and of course I had to get one of their homemade pastries to go with it. You really don't get the full flavor of iced coffee without something sweet on the side. I walked in my office and turned the thermostat down a notch as a preemptive strike on the day's heat. When I turned around Eunice Favors was standing in the door.

Eunice and I went to high school together. She looks exactly the same as she did then. She's only about five feet tall. I don't have a clue to how much she weighs. With those big baggy sweaters she wears over pleated skirts, who can tell? Today, I suppose in concession to the heat, she wore a lightweight sweater vest and T-shirt over her skirt. With her bobbed hair cut, square bangs and large-framed glasses, she's always reminded me a little of Velma from the Scooby Doo cartoons.

Her parents are what folks around here refer to as "trailer trash." I don't like the label. Lots of really upstanding people live in manufactured homes. But even I had to admit the Favors clan *was* a little trashy. Their particular trailer resides on a patch of land on the outskirts of town. Mr. Favors and Eunice's brother Art are shade tree mechanics and their "lawn" is always littered with cars and car parts.

Mrs. Favors didn't seem to do much of anything except voice her complaints at every school board, PTA and town council meeting. She always acted as if every rule or law was made to discriminate against her and her family. When the boys got in trouble with the law for minor infringements, she was sure they would not have been charged if their names had not been Favors.

Eunice never quite fit in with the rest of her family. She was a year ahead of me in school. She was a real bookworm, but had lousy grades. Eunice was always reading books, but they weren't the ones the teachers assigned. We had a couple of classes together, and she was forever getting in trouble for reading. She'd be reading *Catcher in the Rye* instead of dissecting her frog in biology. The geography teacher took *Zen and the Art of Motorcycle Maintenance* away from her because she was reading it instead of drawing her map of Africa. (Mrs. Favors was sure the teachers gave her poor grades because of her last name. After all, how could a teacher object to a student reading too much?) And just forget about math. I had geometry with Eunice my sophomore year when she was a junior. I don't think she ever turned in a single assignment.

Somehow she managed to graduate and get into a local junior college. I guess she figured out which books she ought to be reading, because she went on to the University and got a degree in library science. She landed the rather plum job as the Hilltop librarian about six years ago when Addy McGuire retired. Now she reads whatever she wants.

"Sorry to just show up unannounced, Lu," she said softly. Eunice is the town librarian. She almost never speaks above a loud whisper.

"It was rather rude of me, but I really needed to talk to you."

I waved at her to sit down.

"Oh, don't think anything about it," I told her. "Fortunately, business is slow right now. I'm not busy at all. What do you need to talk about?"

"It's about the Magnolia Club," she said and sighed loudly.

I just waited.

"You know after Mrs. Street died, it left an opening in the club," she began to explain. "Most of the women in the club use the library regularly, and they all know me. Several of them nominated me to be the replacement.

"I was so excited," she continued. "Me! A member of the Magnolia Club. The club that started it all west of the Mississippi. Who knows if there would even be book clubs if it hadn't been for those original members. But then, Mrs. Terwilleger came by the library and told me she was so sorry, but the vote had not been unanimous and they just couldn't accept me. I was devastated. I didn't know if it was one person or several who ousted me. But I heard Miz Maddie talking to Mrs. Whirley at the market the other day saying what a shame it is that the woman who knows more about books than anybody else in town is being kept out of the Magnolia Club by the member who never reads the books. That has to be Lettie Gibbs."

I gave Eunice a look that signaled that I was shocked, but I wasn't really. My aunt is a snob who needs to look down on other people. What would it say about her to be a member of a club that included the likes of the daughter of a lowly mechanic?

"I know we're not real close, Lu," she said, so softly I almost couldn't hear her over the hum of the air conditioner. "But I wondered if maybe you could talk to your aunt and get her to change her mind. They haven't filled the spot yet, and it would just be a dream come true for me to be a member of that club."

I looked at frumpy little Eunice and made my decision right there and then.

"Eunice," I said as I stood up. "You, more than anyone else I know, deserve to be in that club. My aunt is not a bad person, but she is slightly misguided. I think I can put her back on the right track. I can't guarantee anything, but I'll lay odds that you'll be at the next meeting of the Magnolia Club."

I thought she was going to cry.

"Oh thank you so much Lu. Nobody's ever done anything like this for me. I will be forever in your debt. You'll never pay a fine at the Hilltop Library again."

Now that was something coming from Eunice. She's a little militant about getting books turned in on time.

As soon as Eunice left, I picked up the phone and dialed dear Aunt Lettie.

She answered with a characteristic "Bon jour!"

"Letitia," I started, foregoing any courtesy titles. "I've just received a visit from our esteemed town librarian. She claims that you are keeping her out of the Magnolia Club. Is that true?"

There was a short pause before she responded.

"Now, Lu, she said. "Don't go getting on your high horse. The Magnolia Club is an historic organization. We have standards to uphold. Eunice is a perfectly lovely person, but even you have to admit that her family is downright common. No, Lu. It just wouldn't do to have the Favors name associated with our club. Surely you understand."

"No," I said. "I don't understand at all. Eunice deserves to be in that club. At least she would actually read the books!"

"Now, Lu. There's no cause to get surly."

"Oh, I won't get surly. I'm going to get chatty. If you don't go to the next meeting and tell the rest of the members of the club that you've reconsidered your stance on Eunice, then I will be forced to tell what I know."

"Oh, Lu. You wouldn't dare!"

"I'd hate to do it. But you would leave me no choice."

"Well!" she huffed. "I can't believe that I am being blackmailed by a member of my own family. I could be ruined and you don't even care."

"I think you may be being a bit dramatic, but nevertheless, I'll do it. I'll tell Ms Maddie today, and by Sunday everyone in town will know."

"All right. Okay. I'll do it," she finally conceded. "But don't expect to be eating any of my cooking anytime soon!"

And with that snappy little comeback she hung up on me.

Well, a break from Aunt Lettie's cooking can only improve my waistline.

Lest you think I am a horrible person for doing what I did to my own aunt, I'll let you in on the big secret.

When I worked in St. Louis, my boss, Hope, was a former sorority sister of Letitia's at William Woods. William Woods girls are supposed to be the epitome of grace and manners, but apparently, my aunt was quite the party girl. Stephens College, the nearby boys' school, held a big pig roast at the end of every school year, and for three year's running, my Aunt Lettie won the beer chugging championship—downing a record 72 ounces in three minutes in her senior year. Hope even had a picture of Lettie showing off her first-prize ribbon. Hope didn't really care about keeping the picture, and when I asked for a copy of it, she gave me the original. Surely the fates intended it to be used to bring a little justice into the world.

Anyone else would have chalked the whole episode up to the folly of youth, but Aunt Lettie was scandalized that I knew about her "wild oats." She made me swear not to ever tell a soul. Like I said before, I normally would never use what I know to damage anyone's reputation, but if threatening my prissy Aunt could make Eunice's dreams come true, then my moral fiber could stand a little unraveling.

Anne Russ and Nancy Russ

CHAPTER 30

It was the day I'd dreaded since I moved back to Hilltop. Dreaded almost in a hypothetical sort of way, since I never really believed that what I dreaded could ever actually come to pass.

It was my day off and Jim Pat and I were painting my bedroom. We were actually only painting one wall—dark, brick red. I had seen it done in a magazine a couple of months ago and loved the effect. So Jim Pat had been recruited to help move furniture, cover carpet and bring his power paint roller—there are so many reasons to have a man around.

We had finished about a quarter of the wall when the phone rang. It was Mo.

"Lu, I think you should get down here right away," he said quietly. I didn't pick on up anything—Mo always speaks in kind of a hushed voice.

"Oh, Mo, can't Grandpa handle it," I begged. "It's my day off, and I'm up to my ears in a custom blend of burnt rouge and muted scarlet."

"Lu, the call is Grandpa," he said softly—even more softly than before.

I couldn't speak. It was the most bizarre feeling. All these thoughts and images were bombarding my brain, yet I couldn't seem to form a single syllable with my mouth.

"Lu? Lu," I heard Mo saying. "Is Jim Pat there with you?"

I managed to croak out a "yes."

"Have him bring you to the office," Mo said. "As soon as possible. OK?"

"Okay."

I put the phone down and turned around to see Jim Pat staring at me.

"Gosh, Lu, what is it?"

"Grandpa," was all I could get out before the tears started to flow. Before any one of them hit the ground, Jim Pat had his arms around me. I sobbed and sobbed until his shirt was soaked through, and I was out of tears. For a few brief moments—all cried out and in Jim Pat's

133

arms—I felt like everything was going to be all right, but as soon as I let go, I knew nothing would ever be all right again.

Twenty minutes after Mo called I was still trying to pull myself together. I knew Mo was waiting for me, so I sucked it up and handed Jim Pat my keys. We just left everything right where it was. Jim Pat did have the presence of mind to put the lid on the custom-mixed gallon of paint.

Jim Pat kept one hand on mine as he drove me to the office. He didn't say anything. I couldn't say anything. I was trying to make sense of what was happening to me. I was numb with grief. How could that be? I've always known Grandpa couldn't live forever. In fact, most of us couldn't believe he had lasted this long. I still couldn't make him be gone in my head.

"He's left me, too," was all I could think. Twenty years of anger at my mother were bubbling up from somewhere inside me and being directed at the wonderful man who was the one person I have always been able to count on. After Mom left and Dad was merely going through the motions of life, it was Grandpa who was always there for me.

It just dawned on me in the car, riding over to the funeral home, that Grandpa never once made a disparaging remark about my mother. Here was a woman who had left his son and granddaughter, and he never spoke ill of her. I still remember what he used to say to me when I would ask why she left.

"It had nothing to do with you, Lu. It wasn't your fault. Sometimes folks have their reasons for doing things that other folks won't ever understand. There was nothing you could do to stop it. There's nothing you can do to change it. You just have to find a way to live with it."

All of a sudden we were pulling up to the funeral home. I have no idea how we got there. I mean, I realize Jim Pat drove us there, but I didn't remember the route at all. Mo was waiting for us at the door.

"He died at his desk," Mo said, hugging me and not letting go. "I was working in the back, and I came in to ask him a question about the deceased. He looked like he was napping in his chair. I even kind of smiled to myself thinking that Grandpa was finally acting his age. When he didn't wake up, I went over and touched his hand. I knew right away. I called Doc Green as soon as I hung up with you. We've moved him into the visitation room. I didn't want you to see him in the preparation room."

He smiled weakly. "Who else but Grandpa would have the good sense to die right in the middle of a funeral home?"

Mo finally released his grip on me, and suddenly realizing that Jim Pat was present, embraced him as well. Mo is not a touchy-feely kind of guy, but if this sudden show of affection surprised Jim Pat, he didn't show it. He hugged right back and kept his arm around Mo while he held my hand as we walked into the funeral home.

Doc Green was standing in the foyer. "As far as I can determine, his heart just stopped," Doc said, reaching to take my hand. "There's no reason to do an autopsy, unless you'd like one done. We generally don't do autopsies on 93-year-olds unless there's a curious circumstance surrounding the death."

I just nodded, hoping Doc Green would interpret numb gestures appropriately. I left them all standing in the foyer and walked into the visitation room.

Unlike most of the deceased in this room who have had the benefit of Mo and Emily's skills, Grandpa did indeed look dead. His skin had taken on an unnaturally pale hue and even his skin seemed slack and dull.

I've seen hundreds of people speak out loud to corpses in this very room. I've always found it odd, since I consider a person's dead body to be a separate entity from the person who once inhabited the body. So I didn't vocalize what I needed to say to Grandpa. I said what I needed to say inside my mind with my head bowed and eyes closed— almost like a silent prayer to Grandpa.

"How could you go and die on me? Mo and I can't run this place without you—not like you did. We can't be you. You were the best, Grandpa. The absolute best. We're going to miss you something terrible."

Okay, so it wasn't like any prayer I've ever heard, but I still maintain that I was not carrying on a conversation with a dead person. I wouldn't do that.

I went to my desk and got out the sealed envelope Grandpa had given me on my one-year anniversary with Gibbs. It read "in case of my death." Grandpa is one of the few people in this world who had a sense of humor about his own mortality. I opened it up and found a letter.

Dear Lu,

If you are reading this, then despite my extensive experience in dealing with Death, I have been unable to outwit him. Don't be sad. Few people can boast the kind of life I have been fortunate enough to lead.

I'm leaving the funeral home to you and Mo. It's split between the two of you fifty/fifty. You have far more assets than liabilities. I have seen to that. Do with the funeral home what you will. If at some point, you and Mo decide that this is not the life for you, don't feel that you owe it to me to continue on. Having my two grandchildren come into the business and work with me in my final years is more than any man could ask for. All I truly want now is for you to be happy.

The house already belongs to your father. I have split my personal assets between my two sons, and left cash bequests to you, Mo and Francois. But that's all in the will.

Instructions for my funeral are in an envelope under that blotter on my desk. Harry Thatcher in Stuttgart and I have had a long time agreement that whoever lives the longest will direct the funeral of the other. Don't know what Harry will do about his own funeral now, but I guess it's not my problem anymore.

Lu, you are a smart, compassionate, beautiful woman, and I'm so very proud of who you have become.

Love,

Grandpa

The next couple of days were sort of a blur. Mo insisted on preparing the body, but I let Thad and Mr. Thatcher handle the rest of the funeral service preparations. My need to be in control was completely washed away by grief.

It took all the strength of character I could muster to deal with the throngs of people who laid siege to my father's house. The requisite "condolence food" came as expected. Even with the many mourners who gathered at our house, I still had Jim Pat take several casseroles and cobblers over to our local battered women's shelter.

And then to listen to the words of condolence! All this time in the funeral business, and I never knew how maddening it was. If one more person told me, "He had a good life," or "It's all for the best," "Be grateful he didn't suffer," or the worst—"It was his time"—I was going to scream. I didn't care what his life was or wasn't, or what the hell time it was! All I cared about was that he wasn't here now!

I know people were talking about me. I'm usually the poised, in-control person in this kind of setting. But for this particular funeral, I didn't feel like being sociable. Daddy and Uncle Billy were handling it well, under the circumstances. Aunt Lettie played the perfect hostess and tried to explain why I wasn't being my usual self.

At the funeral there was a time for people to stand up and give their own personal eulogies. The first couple were very touching, but so many people opted to do their own eulogizing that it got a little long and my mind began to wander. How on earth will Mo and I manage the funeral home? Will Daddy and Uncle Billy want to get involved now that Grandpa is gone? Should we shut it down? And...who the hell sent those carnations? There they were, a huge arrangement of white carnations—it had to be the largest bunch of flowers in the chapel. Grandpa hated carnations—filler flowers, he called them. Some casket sales rep must have sent them.

Finally, the personal eulogies were over, and Thad took the podium.

"Friends, this is a sad occasion indeed. It's not sad for Ernest P. Gibbs. Looking around the room, I feel it is safe to say that all of us believe in the Resurrection and the Life, and that Mr. Gibbs is in Heaven right now looking down on all of us. And Ernest himself often said that he was blessed with a life better than any man deserved.

"In Thornton Wilder's play, *Our Town*, someone asks, 'Does anyone ever realize life while they live it—every, every, minute?' And the town philosopher answers, 'Saints and poets, maybe.'

"I don't know whether Ernest qualifies as a Saint or a Poet—maybe both—but I can say that he came as close as anyone I have ever known to living life to its fullest.

"No, it is not a sad day for Ernest Gibbs.

"But it is a sad day for all of us. Because I feel it is safe to say that everyone in this room at one time or another was comforted by Ernest Gibbs. His gift was almost magical. At some of the lowest points of our lives—the loss of a loved one—it was Mr. Gibbs who was there with a kind word, a warm touch and a sympathetic ear. Surely there were others who offered the same kinds of comforts, but Ernest Gibbs was different. There was something in those eyes—just being in his presence made you feel a little bit better. Even when things were at their darkest, Ernest Gibbs could make you feel like the light just might shine again.

"So, it is sad for us to know that the next time we are facing that sort of grief, Ernest Gibbs will not be here. It is sad for us to know that we will not see him on a day-to-day basis. For even when life is going well, this was a man who could make it seem a little bit better. Let us pray."

After the service, we all went back to the church where the WOC had prepared lunch for everyone. About 500 people crowded into the fellowship hall to munch on sandwiches and potato salad. The food/death connection is hard to break.

Jim Pat was standing next to me, holding my hand, and I had plastered a benign smile on my face and merely nodded at everyone who came by to offer condolences. I looked at a table full of "mourners" chatting away merrily about this, that and the other like they hadn't just come from a funeral. "Hello, people!" I wanted to scream. "A man is dead here. Am I the only one who cares?"

Just when I thought my head was going to explode, Mo did something extremely out of character—something I had never seen him do before. He stood up, clinked his spoon on a glass and asked for everyone's attention. He got it.

"Um, thank you all for coming. Grandpa would be honored that you all came today. He considered you all to be his friends.

"Um, I also think he would like it if I took this time to make an announcement. I told this to Grandpa the day he died. Since then, it didn't seem right to bring it up, what with all of us mourning his loss. But Grandpa always did like to temper bad news with good, so I decided he would think that this sad day is the perfect place to share some good news.

"For reasons that I have yet to understand, Emily has consented to be my wife. Grandpa was thrilled with this news, and I hope you all are too."

Emily, who was at his side, was red with embarrassment, but smiling from ear to ear.

Everyone paused for a moment, but then someone started clapping. And then everyone was clapping. Soon Mo and Emily were surrounded by well-wishers shaking their hands and giving them hugs. Everyone acted as if Mo and Emily getting married was the most natural thing in the world. I looked at Jim Pat.

"Where have I been?" I asked. "Mo and Emily? When did this happen? Have they even been dating?"

"Gee, Lu," Jim Pat said. "Only about every time someone in this town died. Don't you realize how much time they've spent together over the last two years? I can't believe you, of all people, are surprised at this news."

"Well, I am. I had no idea. Mo's a great guy and Emily is about the cutest and sweetest thing on earth. I just never thought of them as a couple. But apparently, I was the only one."

I pushed my way through the crowd to get to the happy couple.

"Maurice Gibson!" I scolded. "How dare you do something as all-fired important as getting engaged and not even clue your favorite cousin in on it? If you've set a date too soon for me to give the two of you a proper engagement party, I just may never forgive you!"

Mo's troubled face broke into a smile when he realized how happy I was for him and Emily. And I was truly happy. An hour ago I wasn't sure that I would ever be this happy again.

Then I began to see other people in the crowd. Aunt Lettie was standing close to Uncle Billy—and they were talking to Francois and his friend Tim! For the first time, I worried about Dad, but then I found him. Glenda was holding his hand.

Janice came over to give me a hug, and Harley was beside her, looking handsome in a dark suit. Karen and Bill were there, of course, and Rebekah and Jon Bennett were with them. After Rebekah gave me her obituary, her parents decided to send her to California for some alternative treatments. And they worked! Her cancer is in remission, and although they say it could come back any time, she's taking life one day at a time. That's really all any of us can do, isn't it?

Suddenly I realized I had had this feeling before. Mo's announcement was like the sunrise after Jim Pat's sister's funeral. The very worst thing in the world that could happen had happened. Grandpa was gone. But Mo's news brought me back to the realization that the rest of us are still here. And we are going to be okay.

I found Jim Pat in the crowd, and right there in the middle of the fellowship hall at the Calvary Baptist Church I planted a good ten-second kiss right on his lips. Before he could recover from the shock of my very public display of affection, I grabbed his hand.

"Come on, sweetie," I said. "Take me home."

ABOUT THE AUTHORS

Nancy and Anne Russ are a mother-daughter writing team. Nancy grew up in small towns in the south and got her first job with a weekly newspaper when she was 16. Although she has had a number of different jobs since then, writing and teaching have dominated her career. She lives with Anne's father in Little Rock, Arkansas.

Following in her mother's footsteps, Anne has worked as a writer and magazine editor. She now lives with her husband and daughter on a seminary campus in Massachusetts where she is preparing for the ministry. Because they are abundantly blessed with wonderful relationships, the Russes have attended and even conducted (with the help of their husband/father) more than their share of funerals.